I0691393

LEATHER NAZIS

First Edition

Published by The Nazca Plains Corporation
Las Vegas, Nevada
2009

ISBN: 978-1-935509-52-3

Published by

The Nazca Plains Corporation ®
4640 Paradise Rd, Suite 141
Las Vegas NV 89109-8000

PUBLISHER'S NOTE
Leather Nazis is a work of fiction created wholly by *G.W. Leatherman Parks'* imagination. All characters are fictional and any resemblance to any persons living or deceased is purely by accident. No portion of this book reflects any real person or events.

Cover Photo, Fleshblack
Art Director, Blake Stephens

DEDICATION

To Jim,
a willing Leather submissive,
an affectionate Leather pup,
a novice cigar smoker,
who knows how to accentuate
the correct Leathered parts
and recognizes a handsome chest.

All lead to our mutual Leather pleasure.

DISCLAIMER

This book is clearly a work of fiction. I do not support the atrocities committed by Adolph Hitler and members of the Nazi party. Like many Leathermen, however, the uniform and knee-high boots worn by members of the party attract me as a man of Leather. It brings into play the respect and fear people feel when they see a man in full uniform marching authoritatively down the street. The power play between an emotionless man and his submissive boy is explored in this work and in my mind was most effective when portrayed during the Nazi regime. It could have been a uniformed cop, a United States Marine, or a biker in full black Leather. It also brings into play the animalistic qualities that we all share, normally suppressed, in our sexual appetites, most primarily in the world of Sadomasochism.

LEATHER NAZIS

First Edition

by the black Leather gloved hands of
G.W. Leatherman Parks

CONTENTS

CONTENTS CONTINUED...

CHAPTER ONE

Leather Nazi

Gunther Meissner entered Der Fuehrer's army the day after he turned twenty. He had no real desire to be in the military, but was seeking his Father's approval. His Father was an Officer in the SS, high in the ranks. From early childhood, Gunther desperately wanted his Father's approval, but never seemed to receive it. His Father was cruel and stern and Gunther, the only boy, received more than his share of punishment, from slaps across the face to firm beatings on his ass. Gunther had grown into a tall young man, well-qualified as a member of the Aryan race. Blonde hair, blue eyes, athletic body.

Despite the fact that he was an Officer's son, he received little if any special treatment. Within days of his enlistment, he was sent to a training camp for instruction. A review of the new recruits was announced for 1800 hours. And Gunther, along with the rest of the recruits, was hustled into the yard of the camp.

Karl Roebling was the commanding officer and from what Gunther had heard that afternoon, he was one to be feared.

1

"ACHTUNG." The soldiers were called to attention as the Commandant made his appearance. He cut an impressive figure, marching toward the boys in goose-step precision with his staff. He ranked even higher than Gunther's Father.

He wore a black Leather uniform. Shined boots to the knee, black Leather breeches, and military jacket. Leather shirt with a precisely-tied tie. Swastikas on each lapel. Even his red armband with the swastika was made of the finest Leather. Black Leather gloves so supple you could see the flexed knuckles of his hand, which held a black Leather riding crop. The crop sported a silver tip with his monogram. The crop, for the moment, was tucked under his arm. However, it had been used on many occasions to alert a soldier of his misconduct or transgression. Commandant Roebling enjoyed using it.

Gunther's knees felt that they would buckle in the presence of this powerful man.

Commandant Roebling stood and faced the recruits, his legs spread apart, his Muir cap shading his eyes.

"Sieg Heil! I am Commandant Karl Roebling. You will address me as Commandant or Sir. I tolerate no improper conduct within this camp – you will be sought out and severely punished." He continued a whole litany of rules and regulations. The boys listened closely. When he had finished his pronouncements, he marched to the end of the line to review the recruits. The riding crop often struck the cheek of one of the young men. "Your boots look like someone shit on them. Polish them, boy." "Your tie is crooked, asshole." "Don't look in my eyes unless I tell you to look in my eyes, boy" As he approached Gunther, the young man was even more nervous. "What will be my transgression?" he thought.

"Well, well, well, who do we have here?" the Commandant questioned as he approached the young man. Gunther's light blue eyes stared straight ahead.

"Gunther Meissner, Mein Commandant," he barked in what he hoped was a steady voice.

"Yes, Meissner. The unruly boy. I have heard of you through your Father." With that, Gunther was lashed twice across the cheek, drawing blood, "Don't think you will get any special treatment from me because of who your Father is, boy."

The Commandant continued, but at least Gunther's inspection was over for the moment.

The Commandant returned to his private quarters. He propped his feet up on his mahogany desk and pulled out a crystal decanter with one glass. He reached into a hidden drawer and pulled out a Cuban cigar. As he puffed the cigar, he massaged his Leather breeches. He reviewed the troops in his head. Most of them were average looking, but that Meissner boy. 'Handsome', he mused as he continued to puff on his cigar. "I'll bet he has a nice cock in his pants," he surmised, as he continued to rub his cock through his uniform. He unbuttoned his breeches and extracted his erect cock.

"REINHARDT! Get your ass in here...," the Commandant bellowed.

His trusted aide appeared in the doorway. He pretty much knew what the Commandant wanted but waited to be told to crawl under the desk and service the commanding officer's member.

Reinhardt positioned himself under the desk as the Commandant stroked his hardening cock. His cock was long and slender, but a goodly size. Reinhardt took it in his mouth and swabbed the shaft up and down. While Reinhardt was servicing his Commandant's manrod, a second aide knocked, requesting entrance.

"Sieg Heil! Mein Commandant, these directives just came from Der Fuehrer's headquarters. To be processed immediately." He exited.

"Fuck the Fuehrer, I need my cock serviced first," mumbled Roebling as he pulled Reinhardt's head closer to his crotch.

After a length of time, the Commandant reached climax. The residue of cum on his cock was quickly lapped up by

Reinhardt who then quietly left as the Commandant shuffled through the paperwork.

The boys were put through hell in their weeks at camp.

Gunther wanted nothing more than to survive without further incident, but it seemed impossible.

The Commandant singled Gunther out more than once for infractions, both real and seemingly imagined.

Gunther bore them silently, rarely talking to the other recruits about the barrage of beatings inflicted upon him by the Commandant.

About three weeks after they had arrived, Reinhardt threw open the door, "ACHTUNG!" The soldiers snapped to attention as the Commandant marched into their bunkhouse.

"Werner and Meissner, you have one hour to pack your kit for weekend maneuvers."

The two boys hastily put together their essentials and reported to the Commandant's private office.

"Sieg Heil, Mein Commandant" as the boys saluted their commanding officer. He returned the salute.

He did not offer them a seat as this meeting would be brief. He, however, sat in his chair, propped his feet on the desk, and lighted a cigar.

"I have been called to a military council meeting in Dresden for the weekend. I need two assistants to serve as my aides and I have chosen the two of you."

"Thank you, Mein Commandant, it would be an honor..." said Claus Werner.

Gunther echoed the thanks but with less conviction in his voice.

"Meissner, you seem hesitant. Is there a problem of which I am not aware?" His eyes twinkled.

"Nein, Mein Commandant, it would be my extreme honor to accompany you."

By now, a large touring car, emblazoned with Nazi flags had pulled up in front of the Commandant's quarters.

The driver saluted the Commandant and opened the door for him. Claus Werner started to crawl into the back but was rebuked.

"Nein, Werner, you will sit in the front with the driver. I wish to speak to Herr Meissner alone." A glass divider separated the two compartments – the conversation would be private.

As the car entered the roadway, the Commandant took several puffs on his cigar before turning to Gunther.

"I wanted to talk to you, boy. You have a special quality not unlike your Father. I think you have a potential to rise through the ranks in the SS."

"Thank you, Sir."

"I could help you with the advancement, boy, but you will have to obey my every order," the Nazi officer continued.

"Yes, Sir"

The Commandant continued to stoke his cigar. He began rubbing the front of his pants with the handle of his riding crop. At first, Gunther did not pay much attention, but as the man's cock became more and more stimulated, it made its presence known in the tight breeches the Commandant wore.

Gunther looked out the window.

It gave the Commandant a chance to look at the boy. The boy was tall – his booted feet stretched across the floor of the sedan. His jacket outlined his muscular torso. Before the boy had turned his face, the Commandant had memorized the aquiline nose, the light blue eyes. "Handsome," he once again concluded as his erect cock continued to respond to the rubbing of the Leather riding crop and thoughts of having the boy between his legs.

"In profile, boy, you look like your Father. He is proud to be serving in Der Fuehrer's military."

"Yes, Sir, I know," the boy responded, "it is why I joined." As the boy continued to look out the window, his eyes welled with tears. The boy blurted out, "I want to make my Father proud of me."

"Rest assured, boy," the Commandant crooned, "I will put in a good word for you as long as you obey me."

The boy shook his head and turned to face the Commandant.

The Commandant had unbuttoned his breeches and was gripping the shaft of his enlarged cock in his gloved hand.

The boy gasped.

"Relax, boy, we all play with ourselves. It relieves the pressures of the day. Even Der Fuehrer is known to wank off. Although, I know on good authority, he doesn't have much of a cock. He's not of the Aryan race, boy, he is not like you and me." The Commandant now had gray hair, but his mustache still showed blonde hairs among the gray.

"Your first order, boy, is to take my cock in your hand and rub the entire shaft of the cock with your gloved hand."

"No, I won't do it, you disgusting pervert."

The Commandant temporarily stopped rubbing his cock and lashed out with his riding crop. It struck the boy's face repeatedly, drawing blood very quickly.

"SHITHEAD..." yelled the Commandant. He pulled the boy closer to him by grasping the lapels of his uniform and thrust his tongue down the boy's throat.

The boy struggled but he was pinned down in the corner of the sedan by the Commandant's body. The Commandant continued rubbing his extended cock while tonguing the boy's throat.

The Commandant shot a load of jism all over the vehicle's seat.

"Lick up my cum, you asshole, or I will let it be known that you are of impure blood and you will be sent on one of the trains. It would disgrace your family, especially your Father. Now, lick it up before I order the driver to stop."

The boy felt he had no choice but to obey and with that, licked up every drop of the Commandant's manjuices.

Not having tasted cum before, the boy was surprised that he enjoyed its taste. "This is what a real man's cum tastes like," he thought.

The Commandant patted the boy's head as the boy licked the cum off the sedan's Leather upholstery.

Soon after, the sedan pulled into the compound. The driver opened the Commandant's door and the officer and his boys entered the building.

The Commandant was whisked off to a private meeting, and the boys were allowed to relax until needed.

"So, Meissner, what did you and the Commandant talk about?" queried Werner.

Gunther was reticent to reveal any of the activities and just shrugged it off. "Nothing much," he replied.

The boys relaxed in the courtyard, being served coffee by one of the many aides that seemed to swarm around the compound.

After several hours, another aide appeared in the door to the courtyard. "Werner, you are to report to Herr Bruner's office for details of your work assignment. Meissner, you are to report to Commandant Roebling's temporary office. I will direct you." Meissner was led down a flight of steps, down several corridors, and into an office with rich, wood paneling and artwork covering the walls. The Commandant was seated in a chair, his booted feet propped up on a footstool.

"In, Meissner. Close the door behind you."

The boy obeyed and stood at attention.

"Sit down, boy," as his hand directed the boy to the chair next to the Commandant.

The boy obliged.

"A glass of sherry, boy?" as the man handed him a stemmed glass filled with the reddish-brown liquor.

"Taste one of my cigars... you will like it. Recently taken for us from a man of inferior breeding. He won't be needing them any more...." The Commandant chuckled.

The boy kept his thoughts to himself, initially refusing the cigar.

The Commandant insisted and lighted the cigar for the boy. The riding crop was poised as if ready to strike. Gunther was forced to accept it. He thanked the Commandant and admitted to himself that it had a full-bodied flavor.

"Now, boy, let's talk about your duties while here. I will be in a series of meetings throughout the weekend. But, there is time for leisure activity. I will expect you to be ready to 'assist' me." The Commandant took a long puff on the cigar, his eyes twinkling.

Gunther remained silent. He anticipated a list of tasks, but the Commandant was not forthcoming. Instead, the Commandant drew on his cigar, once again rubbing his crotch area with his riding crop.

It was apparent that Roebling's cock was once again aroused. Its head was straining against the black Leather of the breeches. Roebling flicked the riding crop at Gunther's crotch. The tip connected with the head of Gunther's cock, protected only by the woolen fabric of his uniform, and the boy cried out.

"Did I hurt you, boy?" the Commandant questioned, as he displayed a sadistic smile.

"I wasn't expecting it, Sir." the boy replied.

"My personal aide must expect the unexpected, boy. Unbutton your breeches, boy. I want to see what I am dealing with."

The boy hesitated and received a lash across the cheek.

"NOW, boy! I speak perfect German. Pull your cock out of your pants so that I can examine it."

The boy reluctantly unbuttoned his pants and pulled out his cock.

"You are not excited to be in the presence of a high-ranking SS officer? We cannot have that." The Commandant lifted the flaccid cock with his riding crop. He reached over and began massaging the boy's cock with his gloved hand.

The boy moaned. The buttery soft Leather felt wonderful as the Leathered fingers and palm wrapped around the shaft, sliding up and down, massaging the piss slit. Despite any trepidation concerning the Commandant's 'plan', the boy's cock responded. Fully-extended, the cock looked as if it was sculpted from marble with a thick, fat shaft and a large mushroom head.

The Commandant broke into a sweat, although the boy did not notice. He was too involved with his cock being manipulated.

The Commandant recovered and remarked, "Acceptable." With that he withdrew his hand.

"No, please, Sir. It feels so good..." He received several hard lashes across the chest and one aimed at his hardened cock. The boy screamed in pain.

"Put your cock back in your pants, you mongrel. My cock is the only one that matters." With that, he unbuttoned his breeches and his hardened rod sprang forth.

"Down on your knees, boy."

"Whaat, Sir?"

"I speak German fluently, boy. Get down on your knees and suck my pole. NOW! Or you will be lashed front and back, including that piece of meat hanging between your legs. NOW!"

The Commandant released a series of lashes across the boy's back. Even though the boy had his military jacket on, the lashes still hurt like hell.

The boy knelt before the Commandant, between his knee-high boots, and tentatively took the man's cock in his mouth.

The Commandant directed him as the boy had never had a man's cock in his mouth. The Commandant hurled expletives at him for being so inexperienced.

The boy finally succeeded in encompassing the cock's head and shaft with his mouth. He began to tongue the cock vigorously.

"Slow down, Shithead, I want this to last." The boy began a gentler massage. The Commandant groaned, sliding down in his chair to accommodate the boy. He flicked the riding crop across the boy's back just to remind him who was in charge.

The Commandant's pole, excited by the boy's 'massage', climbed down the boy's throat, pulsating and throbbing with its Aryan juices.

The Commandant continued to berate the boy's technique. The boy received innumerable lashings as he tried to please the man. As he tried to get closer to the base of the man's shaft, his hands gripped the calves of the man's boots. The feeling of Leather, his hands rubbing up and down the shafts of the boots, excited him. He could feel his own cock stirring, recovering from the lashing it received.

The boy began to enjoy the activity. He had never had a sexual experience of any kind and this was erotic. He was enjoying intimacy with a high-ranking SS officer, higher in rank than his own Father. He fantasized that he too would be an officer, a confidante of powerful men, including Der Fuehrer himself. And, at last perhaps, earning his Father's approval. His woolen uniform would be traded for a supple soft black Leather uniform like that worn by the Commandant. Worn proudly, commanding respect and fear. Tall, spit-shined boots. Kicking someone when they got in his way. Black Leather gloves. Slapping a boy's face when he was out of line. A Muir cap with the proud emblem of the Nazi regime emblazoned on the front. Black Leather breeches, with his cock hanging down his pants' leg. "Take anything you want. You are a member of the most powerful nation on the earth. You are an inheritor of the regime. You are a member of the Aryan nation," he rehearsed in his mind as he continued to suck the Commandant's cock. He pictured himself in a wood paneled room, seated in a finely-upholstered chair, his feet propped on the back of a lowlife officer. Smoking an expensive cigar, playing with his cock. Having the boy lick his boots, worship his cock. Ordering the dispersal of inferior human beings, to propagate the higher form of life.

His cock-sucking had continued during this musing and apparently the Commandant was pleased with his improved technique.

With his back arched, the Commandant shot a load of his superior Nazi jism down the boy's throat. The boy relished it, tasting the powerful man's seed.

"Good boy," the Commandant pulled the boy's face toward him and thrust his tongue down the boy's throat.

The boy responded more generously.

"Thank you, Mein Commandant. You are of the finest breeding and it is my immense pleasure to service you. I am here for you to command," Gunther said with great enthusiasm.

"Well, the boy has had a change of heart."

"Jawohl, Mein Commandant"

The weekend continued as the Commandant utilized Gunther as his fuckboy. He fucked the boy's virgin hole and Gunther responded enthusiastically. He enjoyed the rawness, the animalistic intensity of it. "I can take anything," he thought as his ass was being invaded by the Commandant's cock. Perhaps his Father's cruelty had prepared him for this. He wanted to be on the other side of the fucking, however. He wanted to rip a boy's hole open. Thrusting his cock down a scared boy's throat. Whipping him with a riding crop, slapping the boy in the face and seeing that look of pain on the boy's face. Hear the boy scream. "I am a member of the Aryan race. We are the superior race – we will rule the world. Mein Fuehrer understands our destiny."

Under the Commandant's instruction, Gunther grew into an exemplary SS officer, he was promoted quickly and often. For one so young, his advancement was meteoric.

The day arrived when he was the Commandant of an impound camp at Ravensbrueck, just like his mentor Karl Roebling. Roebling had been named Commandant of Buchenwald. Meissner's woolen uniform was replaced by a handsome black Leather uniform, tailored by an old man who was then sent to the gas chamber by Gunther himself. He justified his decision, "He was inferior. He tailored my uniform well, but what else was he good for?" Gunther had become hard, his light blue eyes now glared at everyone with glints of steel. They were usually covered with his Muir cap, pulled low over his forehead. He wanted everyone to view the Nazi emblem he wore so proudly. He marched proudly with a riding crop always under his arm. He looked for infractions so that he could lash someone across the face.

Because of the cruelty now ingrained in his personality, Gunther was often called in for raids of suspected traitors — people who were secreting information to the Allies. Traitors were often brought to him because of his unrelenting punishment until the information was forthcoming from the scum who were presented to him for interrogation. His aides disposed of the traitors after the information was given. He never knew all the details — he had no need to.

He was seated in his office when a knock sounded on the door.

"Enter."

"Mein Commandant, we have a traitor just captured... he has been viewed on at least two occasions near the British Occupational Forces."

"Bring the asshole in."

The prisoner was escorted into the room, firmly held on either side by a Nazi. The man was disheveled and dirty. He had apparently been on the run for some time before his capture by the Nazis. He wore the remnants of his SS uniform.

"So, swine, you have been trading secrets to the Allied forces?" Gunther did not look up at the prisoner, his attentions were focused on the endless paperwork sent to him from Der Fuehrer's cabinet.

"I can explain...," the captor started. He attempted to catch the Commandant's eyes, but they were hidden from view by his visored cap.

"Shut the fuck up! Tell us what we need to know and you will be treated more humanely."

The prisoner did not immediately respond which Gunther took as a sign of resistance. Gunther snapped his fingers and the two flanking guards twisted the prisoner's wrists until two distinct snaps were heard.

The man screamed in pain as both his wrists were broken.

"I don't know anything. You are wrong in assuming that I am a traitor. I have been a loyal follower of Der Fuehrer."

"Turn the prisoner around." The guards did as ordered.

Gunther rose from his desk and approached the prisoner. He ordered the man's breeches be pulled down. He began lashing the man's ass with his riding crop. It excited him to hear the crack of the riding crop against the man's flesh. His cock rose quickly in his breeches

"Bend over, asshole. I will show you my loyalty to Der Fuehrer. Ass-fucking you before you are sent to the gas chamber. You will be sent off, implanted with seed from the Aryan nation."

One of the guards roughly covered the man's mouth with a black Leather gloved hand. The traitor had had his chance to confess.

With that, Gunther unbuttoned his breeches, pulled out his cock, and rammed it up the man's hole.

The man screamed. His mouth was uncovered. "All right. All right. The Brits are planning to attack tomorrow night..." The man spewed forth information, quickly recorded by one of the guards. "I know no more. Please..." His mouth was quickly covered again. His ass remained impaled on Gunther's large cock as it swelled inside the man's rectum. At this point, Gunther was more interested in sexual gratification and increased the pumping of his frenzied cock inside the man's hole. Gunther was unrelenting as he continued to thrust his cock up the abused man's asshole. With a final thrust, he climaxed inside the man.

He hated weak men, he despised men who would betray Der Fuehrer when a little pain was exacted upon them.

He pulled his dripping cock out of the ass of the traitor.

"Take this piece of filth away," Gunther ordered the guards.

As the guards were dragging him away, the man begged for his life to be spared. As he turned in one final attempt to plead for his life, Gunther caught the eyes of the man.

It was his Father.

"Execute him. He is good for nothing more."

Gunther sat back down at his desk, lighted a cigar, and continued reading the directives from Der Fuehrer.

CHAPTER TWO

Commandant Meissner

Commandant Meissner was scheduled to arrive at 1300 hours. His reputation for cruelty had spread beyond the borders of the Regime. The Allied Forces knew of his many acts of brutality. Rumour had it that he had ordered the execution of his own Father, accused of traitorous activities.

The sedan pulled into the compound, Nazi flags proudly waving from the front hood. An aide from the compound opened the door and was surprised to see a young man kneeling before the Commandant, his mouth fully engaged on the commander's private parts. He averted his eyes. The Commandant quickly pushed the young man's head away, hastily stuck his cock back in his breeches, and climbed out of the sedan. The Commandant stared at the aide with his steel blue eyes and flatly stated, "Mention what you saw to anyone and I will cut off your balls myself."

The Commandant cut a striking figure. He wore a black Leather uniform, fashioned from the finest Leather in the world. Black Leather boots, polished by the tongues of his young, handsome aides, were buckled at the knee. His breeches were tight, outlining his manrod and his muscular ass. His jacket, shirt, and meticulously-knotted tie all bore the Nazi swastika in gold. A Muir cap pulled low over his eyes proudly displayed the Nazi emblem. Viewers saw the cap before he revealed his emotionless eyes, brought to life only when he was engaged in sadistic activity. It was then that they twinkled.

The Commandant marched toward the offices of the compound.

"Sieg Heil!" he saluted the other men in the office as they snapped to attention.

He was briefed on the prisoner who had been captured three days before. He had revealed nothing to his captors, showing a defiant spirit. The Commandant was certain that he could break the boy's spirit and his silence with his own brand of interrogation.

His aide followed closely behind with a Leather suitcase. The instruments of pain, or pleasure if you were of the same mind as the Commandant. He was ushered into a darkened room where there was a massive wooden table. It was covered in a sheeting of Leather. A handsome young man was stretched on the top, his arms and ankles manacled to the four corners.

The interrogation officer followed the Commandant into the room.

"The swine is Captain Mitchell Franz. U.S. Army. He has revealed nothing as to his mission, but I'm sure you will persuade him...," the officer began.

"Leave us alone!" barked the Commandant.

His bag of toys had been deposited near the table on a chair and the Commandant began to unpack the items, laying them on another nearby table.

His riding crop was already gripped in his right hand.

"So, prisoner," he began as he leaned over the prisoner's face, "you won't tell us the details of your mission?"

"Damned right," the prisoner replied.

16

The Commandant pulled his cigar case from his flap pocket, clipped a cigar and lighted it, and drew on it heavily. He blew smoke in the boy's face.

"That is a fundamental mistake, boy. YOU WILL TALK TO ME!" the Commandant yelled.

"Fuck you," the boy replied.

The riding crop struck the boy's face repeatedly, drawing blood.

The prisoner spit at the Commandant. The spittle landed on the lapel of the Commandant's jacket.

The Nazi let loose with a barrage of floggings on the boy's naked shoulders and chest.

As the Nazi was flogging the boy, he reviewed a very handsome, muscular chest and powerful arms. He realized that the American was not much older than himself. He liked young flesh. His breeches were already tented with an erection. He wiped the spittle off his lapel and smeared it on the boy's face. The Commandant then reciprocated his prisoner's action, spitting the accumulated tobacco juice at the boy's face. It landed on his chin and drizzled down to the boy's chest.

He reached up with his gloved hands and pulled on the boy's nipples. The boy groaned, but remained impassive.

The Nazi twisted and pulled until the boy was arching his back and attempting to pull away from the nipple torture.

It pleased the Commandant as he smirked.

"I'll have your confession in no time at all. You are a weak candidate for my brand of interrogation."

"Fuck you!" the American replied, although his voice was not quite as confident this time.

"You'll break..." the Leather Nazi assured him. He leaned over and looked into the boy's eyes, "You'll break."

All he saw in the boy's eyes was hatred. For the moment.

The Leather Nazi lowered the boy's fatigues and military-issued underwear. A large cock and low hanging balls were surrounded by a bush of brown hair.

The Nazi grasped the boy's genitals and twisted – hard. His gloved hands were like a steel grip and the boy screamed. The Commandant's hardened cock continued to pulse inside his Leather breeches.

He squeezed harder and harder until the boy thought his privates were going to be pulled off. He would not relent. This Nazi bastard would not get the best of him even if it meant he was castrated.

His gloved hand firmly in place around the boy's cock and balls, the Nazi began twisting the boy's right nipple. He alternated, transferring the pain to the other nipple. He began slapping the boy's cock and balls with his gloved hand and then the riding crop. The boy rocked from side to side but remained silent.

He was unrelenting in his grip on the boy's privates, continuing to flog the boy's chest. He reached down and began flogging the tip of the cock. It must have hurt like bloody hell, but the boy still did not beg for him to stop.

The Nazi's cock was throbbing in his Leather breeches and he knew that it was time to reveal his weapon.

He pulled his cock out of his pants and dangled it above the boy's face.

"I have a present for you, you American swine."

"Put it in my mouth and I'll bite that fucking meat off," warned the cocky prisoner.

"Oh, no, boy, I have no intention of putting it in your filthy mouth... I have other intentions." The boy wrestled against his metal restraints because he knew what was coming. The Commandant placed his cock back in his breeches as he sauntered to the door.

The Commandant banged on the door and ordered four guards in.

"Put the prisoner at the end of the table, face down." The guards wrestled the boy into position while the Commandant calmly puffed on his cigar. The boy still had fight in him but was quickly manacled into place.

The guards hovered, but the Commandant ordered them to leave.

The Commandant moved toward the prisoner, grasping the boy's buttocks firmly. He slapped the asscheeks repeatedly until they were nice and red. His riding crop struck the boy's ass repeatedly. The boy reared up but had his head pushed savagely down onto the table.

The Nazi pulled his manrod out of his breeches once again and eased his cock up the boy's hole.

The boy screamed. He received several floggings across his upper back as his interrogator's German pole inched up the boy's rectum. Once inserted, the Leather Nazi thrust it in and out with a frenzied motion.

"Damn, this feels good, boy. Your American hole was meant to be invaded by Der Fuehrer's Army." He laughed as he continued to pump.

The boy was sweating, squeezing his eyes shut tightly, trying to block out the pain.

The Nazi's thighs were banging against the table as he continued the assault. He began to sweat and the sweat dripped from the brim of his Muir cap onto the ass of the victim.

His cock was throbbing, near climax.

"Relent, boy. Tell us the details of your mission and I will let you up after I fuck you."

"Do the worst you can do to me, you Nazi pig," the boy gasped. "I'll go to my grave with the information I know."

The Nazi did not immediately respond – he was too busy achieving climax. With one final thrust which tore into the boy's hole, he shot a load of jism. It kept cumming and cumming, some of it oozing out of the boy's hole.

The Nazi removed his cock, still dripping with his own cum. He marched to the head of the table. He wiped off his cock with his gloved hand and shoved the four fingers of his glove in the boy's mouth. The boy gagged. The Commandant only laughed, rebuttoned his breeches, and exited the room.

The four guards re-entered the room and without comment, flipped the captive over on his back. Tightly manacled once again.

They departed leaving the boy to assess his aching body. Every part throbbed from the invasion of the sadistic German. But his assault was far from over.

The Leather Nazi reentered the room and strode to the head of the table. Once again, he looked into the venomous eyes.

"That was a good exercise and I must say, you filthy swine, you handled it well."

The boy did not reply.

"What, no thank you? You have just been raped by a high-ranking member of Der Fuehrer's legion of admirers. A little gratitude goes a long way," the Commandant taunted as he spit another large wad of tobacco juice into the boy's face.

"Fuck you," the boy said, but with less spirit and less power in his voice.

"I want you to experience a little toy that I have brought with me, for your pleasure and your pleasure only."

With that the Nazi pulled out a vise and placing it around the base of the boy's cock and balls, tightened the vise until the boy once again cried out in pain. His cock and balls were being crushed by the vise.

"Oh, is that too tight?" the Nazi questioned, "Well, then, let me make it a little tighter." He tightened it even more. He twisted the boy's nipples savagely with his gloved hands and struck the boy's chest with the riding crop. The tip of the crop zeroed in on the boy's aching nips.

Satisfied that the boy was in pain, he once again left the room. The boy twisted from side to side, but there was no way the vise would release its torturous grip.

The boy was kept awake most of the night by the guards who came in to taunt him, spit on him, and piss on him.

The Commandant had retired to a bedchamber provided for him. His aide from Ravensbrueck, a young handsome Aryan, accompanied him to the room and helped the Commandant as he slowly removed his Leather uniform. The boy had been ordered to lick the Commandant's boots. After receiving the Commandant's approval for a job well done, he serviced his Commandant's cock and was then dismissed for the night. As the Commandant lay in bed he replayed the delicious details of the interrogation. He slept soundly, knowing that he had made progress for Der Fuehrer in exacting the details of the boy's role in the maneuvers planned by the American forces. Tomorrow would be a ball-breaker, one way or another. The Commandant chuckled evilly before drifting off to sleep.

He dreamed briefly of the last few moments of the encounter with his Father before his Father was dragged away.

"Did my actions make you proud of me, Papa, showing no mercy on you? The way you showed no mercy to me as a boy. Your boy is a proud member of the Nazi Regime. Soon, you will be all but forgotten but I shall be remembered for a long time." His Father's image faded from his subconscious and the German Nazi slept soundly.

A knock sounded on his door and the young Aryan entered with a breakfast tray. The boy was devilishly handsome and smiled at his Commandant as he approached the bed.

"Good Morning, Mein Commandant."

"You know what to do, boy," the Commandant replied as the boy crawled between the man's stretched legs. His cock was quickly aroused as the boy moistened the man's shaft with his full lips.

The Commandant devoured his breakfast while the boy devoured his Commandant's swollen cock. Meissner only stopped eating when he reached climax and poured his manjuices down the boy's throat.

After that satisfying interlude, the young Aryan helped the Commandant dress. His uniform hugged his trim body tightly. His cock was aroused by the feel of black Leather. Every detail had to be perfected before the Commandant would make his second appearance within the compound. He had another day of interrogation at hand and his eyes twinkled at the thought.

He marched into the interrogation room. The boy was apparently sleeping, fitfully, his head rocking from side to side. Moans issued from his throat. His cock and balls were swollen, still tightly clamped by the vise. The flogging marks were crusted with dried blood.

The Nazi chuckled as he hovered over the boy. He dandled the riding crop on the boy's aching cock as he pinched the boy's right nipple with his gloved hand.

The boy slowly awoke and frowned when he saw the Nazi pig's face.

"Good morning, young man. I trust that you slept well..."

The boy remained silent, his face grimacing as his body ached from the abuse of yesterday.

"If you are polite to me, I will remove the vise."

"Thank you," the boy mumbled.

"I insist on being addressed as 'Sir'. Now, let's try that again, prisoner."

"Thank you, Sir," the boy answered, spitting out the 'Sir'.

"That was a contemptuous response, you asshole," replied the Commandant as he lashed the boy's cock and balls with his riding crop. The boy screamed in pain.

The Commandant left the room and the four guards entered the room. They flipped him over on the table, the vise pressing into the base of his cock and balls. It hurt even worse than when he was lying on his back.

The Commandant returned, smoking his first cigar of the day. He examined the boy's reddened ass. He gave the asscheeks a few healthy slaps as he removed his enlarged cock from his breeches.

"Time for another assfucking. You are quickly becoming my bitch," taunted the Nazi.

The boy did not respond, as he was trying to keep his privates elevated above the table, in order that the pain was less intense. The Commandant reached under the boy and squeezed the boy's cock and balls. The boy winced with pain. The Nazi continued to rub the boy's asscheeks until he plunged his cock in the boy's invaded hole. He thrust the cock in, back and forth, back and forth. The boy was moaning, but the Commandant did not even hear it – he was too busy concentrating on his own pleasures.

As he continued to pump, a frantic pounding was heard on the door.

"American troops! Storming the compound..." yelled a fellow Nazi. His panicked Aryan boy stormed into the room.

"Mein Commandant, you must flee! The Americans are here... They have heard you are here and are hunting for you. I will take care of the prisoner, you go!"

The Commandant quickly abandoned plugging the boy's hole, his cock hard and throbbing. He exited through a back entrance, known to him and only two or three others. A tunnel connected it to a nearby friendly house where they could then escape to safety.

He crawled through the tunnel which had a number of dead ends and circular pathways. He emerged into the basement of the friendly house, where he carefully wiped off the dust and dirt from his Leather uniform. "Pity," he thought, "I wasn't able to bugger that boy a second time. I know he would have cracked. Shit!"

The commanding officer emerged from the tunnel, followed by one of the guards. The other three apparently had been killed. The Commandant wondered about the fate of his young Aryan boy. He was a good cocksucker. Hopefully he had slit the throat of the American before he himself was killed.

The pounding of footsteps were once again heard in the tunnel as the young Aryan emerged. He brought with him the American prisoner. The Aryan boy had also scooped up the Commandant's toybag and deposited it near the feet of his Commandant.

"I figured you weren't done with the boy, Mein Commandant." The American boy stood before him. Blindfolded, dirty, naked, manacled, and covered with dried blood and whip marks. The vise still gripped firmly on the boy's genitals.

"Good boy," the Commandant announced, "the young man and I have some unfinished business," as he rubbed his crotch with his riding crop.

CHAPTER THREE

Nazi Interrogation

"Damnit, men, how could you fuck up like this?" the American Commander screamed, "He was right within your grasp and you let him go. He just evaporated. And chances are that he still has Mitch Franz with him... somewhere." A botched mission and it would be a permanent stain on his record. The commander swore again. But, it was to no avail. The bastard Meissner had disappeared with one of their top intelligence officers. Mitch knew a lot and it could be a major blow to the Allied Forces if he surrendered the information. It was a stupid idea to plant him within a company of soldiers near the epicenter of action. It was just too damned dangerous. "I knew it," rationalized the Commander, "why in the hell didn't the higher-ups realize it." He only hoped and prayed that Franz was still alive and hadn't succumbed to the Nazi bastard Meissner.

Meissner and the others, along with their American Prisoner of War, were secreted away to a private chalet to reconnoiter with Der Fuehrer and others of the upper echelon.

The prisoner was heavily gagged and manacled as they left the friendly house.

The meeting with Der Fuehrer was brief, but he took special opportunity to thank Meissner and his Aryan aide for bringing in Mitchell Franz. He wasn't a simple Captain it seemed. Their military intelligence told them that he was a higher ranking officer, chockfull of secret information.

Der Fuehrer was impressed with Meissner's past performances and ordered Meissner to continue.

"Mein Fuehrer, it would be my extreme pleasure to continue the interrogation of the American. He will spill all that is inside..., I assure you." Meissner exhibited a sly and sadistic smile as he thought about just what the American would spill. His cock hardened in his Leather breeches, but he suppressed the thought, at least while in the presence of Der Fuehrer. It would be bad form to show a larger cock than Der Fuehrer. Meissner was comfortable in that thought – he knew his cock was larger, he had it on good authority from his fellow Nazi officer Karl Roebling.

As he sat in his private suite at the chalet enjoying a few hours relaxing the Commandant pulled out his cigar case and extracted a Cuban.

He clicked his gloved fingers and his handsome young Aryan came over to clip and light it.

The boy bowed his head as he presented the cigar to his LeatherMaster. The boy worshipped the Commandant and would do anything for him.

He was ordered to kneel in front of the Commandant as the Nazi began massaging his crotch.

It only took him moments to massage his cock into fullness. The man rubbed the boy's head and then pressed the boy's head into the softness of the Leather breeches.

"Sir, it would be my extreme pleasure to taste your cock in my mouth," the boy said hopefully.

"You must be of superior Aryan intelligence, boy, I was thinking just the same thing."

He unbuckled his belt, loosened his pants, and extracted his throbbing German pole.

The boy needed no prompting as he began to tongue the shaft of the cock.

Meissner leaned back in his chair to relax. He began blowing smoke rings toward the ceiling. His thoughts were on the American prisoner.

The cock massage lasted a good thirty minutes. The Nazi was relaxed and thoroughly enjoying it. He wanted to prolong the sucking as long as he could. But viewing that beautiful blonde head bobbing up and down on his cock, and watching the arching of the boy's muscular back and arms was exciting him. "Someday soon, the American Franz will service me just like this," he thought to himself. He detached his riding crop from his belt and began lightly flogging the boy's back. It aroused both the Commandant and his boy. The boy sucked harder and harder until Meissner shot a full load down the back of the boy's throat.

"Thank you, boy, job well-done. Check with the officer to see when I am to have a session with the American." It was obvious that the boy wanted to continue licking up the residue, but he was paddled on the ass and told to obey orders.

He left the room, leaving Commandant Meissner to finger the remaining cum into his mouth.

"Like a good Riesling...," commented Meissner.

A knock sounded and the Commandant's boy entered.

"Sir, the prisoner is ready in Suite B. He is ready for you."

The Nazi checked his appearance in the mirror before exiting the room. He marched to Suite B, where a cross similar to a St. Andrew's Cross was situated. The American was facing the cross, manacled to the four points of the cross. The young man's cock and balls were trussed and sticking through a hole in the center of the cross.

"Well, Good morning, Mitch. Oh, that is your name, I believe. Seems you have been holding out on us. Why,

27

you're no ordinary soldier. We have captured a member of the Intelligence."

The American stood passively. He said nothing, but Meissner knew that he was listening to everything he had to say.

"Well, let's get on with it," Meissner continued as he strode around to the front of the cross. The cross was placed in the exact center of the room for ease of examination and torture.

Meissner reached out and grabbed the American's cock and balls. Even though they were swollen, the boy did not react when Meissner squeezed.

"I admire you, Mitch. Most boys would have flinched."

The American spoke, "With you, I have realized that you get more pleasure out of controlling someone. I am submitting to your control. It doesn't mean I will reveal anything I know – you can beat me, whip me, fuck me, I still won't give you what you want most of all."

"Hmmm," the Nazi pondered the American's statements, "And just what do I want?"

"My spirit."

"Fuck, I want to plow your ass. I want to fuck your throat. I want my Aryan seed dripping down your chin," said the Nazi as he laughed sadistically and lashed the cheek of the boy several times.

The boy calmly replied, "I give you my permission to do so, but you still won't rape my spirit and you won't get the mission details you so badly want. It's obvious that you think you're a meaner fucker than anyone including Der Fuehrer."

The remarks infuriated the Nazi as he began lashing the naked surfaces of the American's asscheeks, his back, and his ribcage. He pulled on the boy's cock and balls, harder and harder.

Oddly enough, the boy remained unflinching. After his tirade had calmed, the Nazi stepped back.

"I have to admire you, Franz. I detract my statements about you being weak. We could use you in Der Fuehrer's Army."

Franz remained silent, but a slight smile was detected on his face.

"Why do you think I allowed myself to be captured?"

"Whaaat the fuck?" the Nazi responded as his jaw dropped.

"Think about it. Did you do any homework on my family background?"

"Well, no...," the Nazi sputtered.

"Franz. Germanic. My father immigrated in 1920 from the Homeland. Worked his ass off to buy a small farm. Loyal as hell to the American government. Public road system came through – Dad wouldn't budge in selling his property, so the fuckers condemned his land. Took it, saying "Fuck you." It broke him. I saw him disintegrate into a bitter old man. Drank, smacked the hell out of my mother and us kids. I vowed then that I'd somehow get even. And this is my chance."

"How do I know that you are telling the truth, you fucking liar?" With that the Commandant, smacked him several times. He got right up in the American's face, "How do I know you are telling the truth?"

"Fuck my ass, again. I'll take it willingly this time. That's how much I want revenge."

The Nazi was puzzled. But the thought of sticking his cock up the boy's ass brought out his sadistic qualities. Even if he was lying, it would be a good assfucking.

His cock had already created a tent in his breeches.

He moved to the opposite side of the cross and pulled out his manrod. It was already throbbing, a drop of dew glistened at the tip.

He held the boy's asscheeks and rammed his cock up the boy's hole. The boy moaned, but it was a soft, "Oh, yes, Mein Commandant, fuck my hole. Ram your German rod up my American ass. Jam it as far as you can..."

The Nazi willingly complied. He pumped it in and out of the boy's ass. He smiled broadly as he continued to feel the thrust of his cock up the relaxed hole.

"Fuck me, Mein Commandant, fuck me!" yelled the American.

The Nazi continued a frenzied fucking, harder and harder, deeper and deeper.

"FUCK!" the two yelled as his load coursed up the boy's ass. He could feel the jism lubricating his dick.

The boy was moaning, twisting and turning as he received the cock and its juices.

Both were sweating as the Nazi pressed his Leathered chest against the boy's naked back. He twisted the boy's tits with his gloved hands. And, in a moment of tenderness, kissed the back of the boy's neck.

"Fuck, Mein Commandant, it all feels so good. I want to be your fuckslave. Keep me here. Fuck me every day."

The Nazi pulled his spent cock out and wiped the jism off with his Leathered glove.

He returned to the front of the cross and inserted his cum-covered glove in the boy's mouth. The boy licked it willingly.

"Well, prisoner. I will take all this into consideration. If you are lying, you will be executed on site – secrets or no secrets. If you are telling the truth, we may have use of you."

The Commandant buttoned his breeches and left the room.

Some time later, two guards took the prisoner off the cross and escorted him to Der Fuehrer's office. Der Fuehrer had been fully briefed of the revelations exacted by Commandant Meissner.

CHAPTER FOUR

A Leather Threesome

The American was interrogated at length by Der Fuehrer. He had his own forms of torture, but suffice it to say the boy was brutalized at the hands of the Nazi leader. The American told him details of the mission which would be checked out for authenticity. Until then, the American would be treated as a Nazi Prisoner of War.

Der Fuehrer called for Commandant Meissner and Commandant Roebling, who had just arrived.

The two men greeted each other warmly in the hallway before marching into Der Fuehrer's office.

"Sieg Heil," as they snapped to attention in the presence of the Supreme Master.

"Sit, Gentlemen." Der Fuehrer clicked his fingers and his personal aide poured a snifter of brandy for each of the men and presented a humidor of cigars.

Each man selected one. The aide clipped and lighted them for the Commandants. They both drew in deeply and exhaled toward the ceiling of the lush office.

"Gentlemen, you already know of the subject. Commandant Meissner has succeeded in loosening up the prisoner. Franz has expressed a willingness to work with us in defeating the Allied Forces. Can we trust him? I'm not so certain – so, we must proceed cautiously, but quickly."

"Jawohl, Mein Fuehrer," replied Roebling. Meissner nodded agreement.

"I want the two of you to take the American prisoner to the estate of an old comrade of mine in Neumunster and work him over. Show him no mercy. See if he breaks. If not, we have a worthy candidate."

"Jawohl, Mein Fuehrer, it would be my special pleasure to do this necessary work for Mein Fuehrer," Commandant Meissner quickly replied, a twinkle in his eye and a sadistic smile forming on his lips.

"You will leave at 1600 hours. Take several guards with you."

"Jawohl. Sieg Heil, Mein Fuehrer." The men left the office and packed their necessary gear.

They reconvened on the patio, awaiting departure.

"Meissner, I hear that you already worked the boy over..."

"Fuck, yes, he is a good fuckboy. Between the two of us, we will rip his ass apart." The men laughed at the impending activity.

A sedan appeared ten minutes before departure and the Nazis situated themselves on either side of the bound prisoner. He was blindfolded, gagged and manacled.

The sedan pulled away from the chalet and in a short time was traversing increasingly rugged terrain. The sedan lurched forward and rocked from side to side as the roads became less well-maintained.

"What a handsome package," remarked Roebling.

Meissner reached over and fondled the American's crotch. "This package is quite nice too. Full of meat."

They began squeezing the boy's crotch and it soon responded. A cock's head was visible beneath the cloth of the trousers.

The cock was soon pulled out of the pants and Leather gloves were stroking the shaft. The boy moaned.

"I've never tasted captured American cock," remarked Roebling and with that he knelt down on the floor of the sedan and tongued the cock's head. Meissner was surprised by this action but not one to miss the action, slid down on the floor and extracted Roebling's cock from his pants. Roebling was greedily slurping the boy's dick while Meissner was tonguing Roebling's extended rod.

Roebling's head continued to bob up and down on the American throbbing cock while Meissner was furiously sucking on his former Commandant's penis. The boy was moaning, his head rolling from side to side as his dick edged closer to ejaculation. Roebling's cock pulsed inside Meissner's mouth.

At that moment, the sedan hit a major pothole in the road and Roebling's head was forced all the way down on the American cock. The boy's cock exploded with a load of jism which Roebling was forced to swallow. At the same time, Meissner's head was jolted and a full mouth on Roebling's shaft made Roebling climax. He shot a forceful load of Nazi cum down the young Commandant's throat.

"Fuck!" both the Nazis intoned as they slurped up the remainder of the cum, "Damn that was good! American cum tastes pretty fucking good!" Roebling declared.

"German cum is superior, Mein Commandant," Meissner remarked as he licked it off his gloved hand and inserted it into Roebling's eager mouth.

"I need to taste more of it to come to a conclusion," Roebling replied as he unbuttoned Meissner's Leather breeches and extracted a throbbing rod. He sucked on the German cock until a thick gob of semen issued forth from Meissner's pisshole.

"Fuck, you're right. But, American cum isn't bad." The two men laughed as they resituated themselves back in the comfortable upholstery of the sedan.

Several hours later, the sedan arrived at the private compound and the driver opened the door for the men. The guards had followed in another sedan and were quick to extract the prisoner from the back seat. The two Commandants marched proudly in their Leather uniforms to the front door.

"Welcome, Gentlemen. I am sure that you will find my home to your liking. Herr Hitler has briefed me on some of your tastes and interests and I am sure you will find it most comfortable." The man who greeted them was the owner of the compound, a rich German who supported the efforts of the SS party. A man of about fifty or so, he was ruggedly handsome, with hair graying at the temples and a trimmed mustache. He, like the officers, was dressed in handsome black Leather. But his was a dress shirt, pleated trousers, and knee-high boots buckled at the knee. He wore skintight black gloves.

"I am Johan von Wiedering." as the men shook his hand. The hallway was filled with artwork and the expensive trappings of a man of wealth. "While your prisoner is being escorted to his enslavement area, I'd like to show you my collection." The Commandants thanked him for his hospitality as he led them throughout the extensive house. Artwork lined the walls.

"This is one of my favorites. It is entitled *The Flogging of St. Paul*. Notice how the blood looks as if it is still oozing from the lashmarks." von Wiedering chuckled. As the Nazis continued, they mutually noted a theme of torture and subjugation.

"How did you acquire these works, Herr von Wiedering?" asked Meissner.

"Herr Hitler and I are close friends. When he comes across an artwork that he thinks may be of interest, he contacts me. I, in return, reward the Party handsomely. Most of the artwork was rescued from persons unworthy of possessing such beautiful pieces. They gave it up willingly... or perhaps not so willingly.

I have elevated it to the worthiness it deserves – admiring it, cherishing it, and on occasion, worshipping it."

The Commandants were aroused by the many depictions, both in painting and in sculpture, of naked men wrestling, men being tortured, men submitting to other men.

"But, Gentlemen, I have offered you nothing to drink." He pulled on a nearby bell pull and a handsome young man appeared from the hallway. He was a beautiful lad, blonde, blue-eyed. He wore Leather wrist and ankle cuffs with large rings attached. His cock and balls hung freely.

"This is Tomas, my boyslave. What would you like, Gentlemen?"

They ordered wine and Tomas disappeared.

He returned shortly with the wine in etched crystal goblets.

As he presented the glass to Meissner, his hand released it a second before Meissner accepted it and the glass crashed to the floor.

"You asshole!" yelled von Wiedering. He pulled open a drawer of an expensive cabinet and pulled out a heavy whip. "Down on the floor, asshole." The boy dropped and von Wiedering administered a series of lashes across the boy's back and ass. The boy whimpered and flinched as the Leather straps cut into his tender hide. Red welts soon appeared on the boy's back and ass.

von Wiedering kicked him with his black Leather boots, cursing at him. "Get Commandant Meissner a fresh glass and then clean this up."

With that, von Wiedering apologized, "He's fairly new. He will pay for that transgression, I assure you."

Neither Nazi said anything. Their cocks had risen in their respective breeches at the sight of another man administering punishment.

The glass was brought to Meissner and they continued their tour of the extensive collection of erotic artwork.

"But, Gentlemen, I assume you would like to view your prisoner's accommodations and then, I will personally show you to your rooms."

The host led them down a lengthy flight of steps to the basement.

As the dungeon came into view, the Nazis were stunned. Every possible torture device imagined was apparent.

The host once again chuckled. "I also collect items of sadism. It has been a long and compelling interest of mine."

He highlighted some of the devices that might be useful in their interrogation.

"My dick is my choice of torture," Meissner thought, but he did not express the sentiment.

The American was chained to a wall. He was still blindfolded and gagged. His clothes had been carefully removed and were neatly folded on a nearby table. His cock and balls were stretched with Leather straps which were attached to a nearby cranking device.

"This is one of my own inventions. I call it the 'Ties that Bind'. As the Leather straps are wound more tightly around the clockwork mechanism it pulls on the subject's manhood. Clever, don't you think?"

The Nazis agreed.

von Wiedering turned the crank several times, pulling on the American's privates. The boy moaned and strained forward, attempting to release the pressure on his manhood. A locking device kept the Leather straps taut.

"Well, Gentlemen, let me show to your rooms. Don't worry, your prisoner will not escape." von Wiedering chuckled once again as he led the way up the staircase. The staircase was accented with two rose marble columns at the top of the landing.

He led them on a brief tour of the second floor where more artworks lined the hallways until showing them to two adjoining bedrooms. Each Nazi was given a room richly appointed with European furnishings and erotic artworks.

"I trust you will be comfortable... ring for my boy if you need anything. Dinner will be in approximately one hour"

Each Nazi viewed his own room. In each room, the four-postered bed was the center of attention. The beds were huge, covered in Leather with Leather pillows. Each of the four posters had rings attached to them.

Each man stretched out on his bed. Meissner planned the session with the American. Roebling revisited the events which took place in the sedan. Both dicks were hard within a short period of time. However, it seemed only minutes before Tomas, the boyslave, knocked on their respective doors and announced that dinner was being served in the dining room.

A veritable feast was served to the Nazis. Both silently wondered who had prepared all the food.

"He must have more handsome boys tucked away," Roebling thought. "I'd like to have them for dessert." But the host did not reveal any other secrets to the Commandants that evening.

The hour was late when they finished their meal and both men excused themselves, returning to their respective bedrooms.

Commandant Meissner was regretting the quick departure from Der Fuehrer's headquarters. His Aryan boy had been left behind. He pulled out his cock and was absently massaging it when a knock sounded on his door. When he opened it, Roebling was standing there. His cock arched out of his Leather breeches. He was shirtless, revealing his finely-tuned, muscular body.

"Thought you might be lonely, Commandant Meissner."

Meissner pulled his former Commandant toward him and his tongue was thrust into Roebling's mouth. Roebling closed the door and walked Meissner toward the bed. They were soon engaged in tugging and pulling at each other's cock. Tongues down each other's throats. So involved were they that they did not hear their host enter the room.

He too had stripped off his shirt and was wearing a Leather hood. His large, handsome cock was throbbing, fully tumescent.

"Mind if I join the party?" the host asked.

He joined them on the bed and reaching around Roebling's waist, unbuckled his breeches and lowered them. He began a moist rimming of Roebling's asshole. Meissner began pulling on his host's cock and balls, slathering them with spit. Roebling, having enjoyed the taste of German cum, began a rigorous sucking of Meissner's low-hanging balls. The Germans continued for some time, trading places often, tasting each other's manhood. Tonguing, spitting, licking, swallowing. Everyone's cock got a thorough workout. Boots and Leather breeches were discarded as asses were explored. Everyone's ass was cleaned with another's tongue before the insertion of gloved fingers. Nips were pulled. Muscles were stroked, massaged, stretched. If a voyeur were present, he would not have been able to tell which arms and legs belonged to which German. The session continued for some time until one cock shot a geyser of cum. It was followed in quick succession by two more geysers. For some time after, there was more licking and stroking. The fuckfest continued long into the night.

Finally, the host stood up. "You will pardon me, Gentlemen, I must attend to my boy. It is time for his nightly whipping."

von Wiedering pulled his Leather pants and boots back on and exited.

The two Commandants lay together in the bed.

Not long after, the crack of the Leather whip could be heard.

The boyslave cried out in pain as each lash struck his back.

The Nazis could not resist. They put their boots on, cocks still dripping cum and exited into the hallway.

The grand staircase which they had walked up was now bathed in candlelight. The two columns flanking the staircase served as posts onto which large chains were now hung. The boy was manacled with wrist and ankle restraints to the columns. von Wiedering, hooded in his black Leather executioner's hood, was positioned behind the boy, a long bullwhip in his black Leather gloved hand. "CRACK! CRACK! CRACK!" sounded the whip as it landed on the boy's ass, back, and shoulders.

The boy's back was already bloodied as he flinched in pain.

The Nazi cocks saluted the efforts of their host.

"Herr von Wiedering, would you allow us to take a few strikes at your boy?" asked Meissner.

von Wiedering handed him the whip and the assault continued. The boy was breathing heavily, his knees buckling, when the assault finally ended.

von Wiedering unbuckled the boy's wrist and ankle restraints and pointed to the floor. The boy knelt in front of his LeatherMaster and began a vacuuming of the man's cock. Once he had satisfied his LeatherMaster, he performed the same service for each Commandant.

Finally, von Wiedering rubbed the boy's head. "Good boy, you have served your Master well. Your transgressions for the day are forgiven." He instructed the boy to go to bed.

Kissing the two Commandants, he also excused himself and the two Nazis returned to Meissner's room. After such a delicious day, they both quickly fell asleep.

CHAPTER FIVE

A Fuck Session in Leather

The two Nazis awoke to a brilliantly sunny day. They had slept soundly and felt refreshed. Both cocks arched upward, full of manpiss. They had only been awake for a few minutes when a light knock was heard on the door.

"Enter," commanded Roebling.

A handsome young man entered, with his head bowed. It was not Tomas. This new boy was wearing similar Leather restraints on his ankles and wrists, his enlarged member and low-hanging balls swinging freely as he approached the bed.

"Sirs, I am Wilhelm, Herr von Wiedering's boyslave. It is my duty to take your morning piss if you so desire for me to take it."

"Well, what a nice service to provide," remarked Roebling as he sauntered toward the kneeling boy.

He pulled the boy's head toward his tap and proceeded to fill the boy's mouth with his cockful. Meissner soon did the same.

"Thank you, Sirs. It is my duty to help you dress if you would so desire for me to do that."

Wilhelm was a good help in getting the men back in their handsome Leather uniforms. And soon, they were ready for the day at hand.

"Sirs, breakfast will be ready in just a few moments on the east terrace." He bowed his head toward them and left the room.

"I wondered if Herr von Wiedering had more than one boy. Now I know," Roebling commented.

Checking themselves in the mirror, the Nazis headed downstairs. They soon found the east terrace breakfast table, laden with a sumptuous meal. Wilhelm quickly appeared behind them to pour their coffee and juice.

"My Master will join you shortly."

The men were admiring the beauty of the estate when Herr von Wiedering appears. Today he was in grey Leather with red piping on the shirt and down the length of the pants. Grey arm gauntlets with red piping and tight black Leather gloves accented his masculine persona.

"Well, Good Morning, Gentlemen, I trust you slept well," von Wiedering remarked as he settled in.

"Very fine, Herr von Wiedering. You are an extremely gracious host," remarked Meissner as he buttered another piece of toast.

"Herr von Wiedering, I am wondering... if you don't mind telling us. How did you accumulate such wealth?" asked Roebling. Curiosity had gotten the better of him.

"Not at all. I inherited quite a bit. But have advanced my fortune...by, um, the human slave trade."

The Nazis, despite their cool demeanors, let out a collective gasp.

"Really, Herr von Wiedering?" questioned Meissner.

The Herr chuckled. "Jawohl. It is true. I have been training and disciplining German youth and then sending them off to like-minded men all over the world. Particularly America. Those bastards have more money than they know what to do with it." He sipped his coffee and continued, "I train the boys like Tomas and Wilhelm and then send them off to serve other sadists like myself. Very lucrative. Every man wants a pretty little boy to fuck."

The men nodded their heads in agreement. Wilhelm reappeared at the table to freshen the coffee cups and remove empty plates. "Wilhelm has been with me for four months. He has been acquired by a rich Australian. He will be leaving me soon." He patted the boy on his naked ass. The boy bowed his head and departed silently.

The men continued to chat until von Wiedering stood up. "Well, Gentlemen, it is time to interrogate your American captive. I have a few duties to execute, but would like to pay a visit to the dungeon a little later."

"Certainly, Herr von Wiedering," assured Meissner.

The Nazis returned to their rooms to gather up a few select toys and made their way to the dungeon. The American's head was lolling to the side. He had been in place for twelve hours or so.

"Wake up, Franz," as Roebling slapped him hard across the face with a gloved hand, "Time for some play, Franz."

With that Meissner and Roebling let loose with a host of floggings from the mean fuckers they had brought with them. Franz's chest and ribcage and upper legs were soon crisscrossed with fresh red markings, laid on top of the marks from previous sessions.

He remained silent.

"You think you are so fucking tough, don't you, you cunt boy!" Meissner yelled.

Despite the punishment he knew he would receive, Franz spit in the face of his captor. He received several backhanded slaps across the face from Meissner.

"Confess, you worthless piece of shit. You aren't going to defect. You were just playing with me, weren't you? You arrogant piece of worthless fuckscum."

"I meant... what... I said," Franz winced as his sentence came out in ragged phrases.

Roebling pulled roughly on Franz's cock and balls. He slapped them with his other gloved hand.

Despite the rough treatment, Franz's cock was hardening. Roebling looked surprised.

"Do...your damnedest... fuck my ass over and over again. I want it. I want your Nazi cream in my asshole."

Roebling and Meissner made eye contact. They nodded in mutual agreement.

They repositioned Franz so that he faced the wall. His ass was still crusted with bloody marks.

Roebling pulled his hardened manrod out of his breeches and obliged the request of the prisoner. He rammed his cock into the receptacle.

"That's right. Fuck me. Fuck me hard, you Nazi swine." That infuriated Roebling and he began ramming his cock in the boy's butt harder and harder. He was sweating from the expended effort.

Meanwhile, Meissner's cock was engorged with German jism. He reached around and lowered Roebling's breeches. Roebling was too concentrative on the boy's hole to take notice until Meissner's cock rammed into his hole.

"Fuck! That feels good, Meissner. Jam it in, fucker."

Meissner obliged. The two began to synchronize their fucking. Cocks pulsing. Growing in length and girth. Throbbing as they reached further and further into the depths of their fuckholes.

Sweat was dripping from all three. Sweat mixed with the smell of warmed Leather. Gasps of pleasure mixed with groans of pain.

The boy was flexing his hands and arms against the stone wall of the dungeon as the Leather Nazis pounded their meat into the warm holes.

As they continued to gyrate in this fuckfest, von Wiedering made his appearance. He quickly pulled out his cock and stood behind Meissner.

Meissner felt his breeches being lowered but couldn't stop his frenzied fucking. Soon, a cock entered his fuckhole.

And the fucking continued.

All four were now drenched in sweat, as the male fuckfest continued. Engorged cocks. Loosened, excited holes.

Male flesh straining, tightening, relaxing. Cockjuice pulsing, ready for an explosion. Balls working overtime in the production of cum. More groans and gasps.

Pumping. Fucking. Thrusts. Animal savagery.

"AAAHH!" as the first man climaxed, quickly followed by two more. The boy, with his cock pinned against the wall, came last. With a lusty scream.

The men were exhausted. They staggered away after pulling their cocks out of the depths of each other.

"Fuck!" yelled Meissner as he sat roughly on the dungeon floor. The two other Leathermen soon joined him.

The American remained manacled to the wall.

CHAPTER SIX

A Leather Confidante

The three Germans adjourned to the east terrace. Wilhelm presented them with drinks and carried with him the humidor as well. After selecting cigars, he clipped the chosen cigars. On bended knee, he lighted each man's cigar beginning with that of his Master.

Wilhelm excused himself in order that the men could enjoy a private conversation regarding the American P.O.W..

Neither German soldier was convinced that Fritz was sincere. Meissner, in particular, was confused. After all, he had given the orders for his own Father's execution. He loathed traitors. His own Father had been one. His Father had been seen with members of the British forces. His own Father who had been a high-ranking officer in the SS. With that knowledge, Meissner felt he must redeem his family name in the eyes of Der Fuehrer.

"He's too much of a risk," Meissner declared, "We should eradicate him. Secrets or no secrets."

"But we need to know what it is he knows," Roebling reasoned.

"I'm tired of the bullshit." Meissner argued.

von Wiedering had remained silent up until this point, "Suppose, Gentlemen, one of you befriends him. Defends him while the other continues to abuse him. Gain his confidence."

"It might work," Roebling conceded.

"I have been unrelenting in my punishment of the swine, so I doubt that he would believe me. Although he did say he wanted to be my fuckslave... Nein, he would never believe that I had softened that much...," Meissner decreed.

"Nothing was soft about you as you plugged my ass," commented Roebling as he rubbed his Leather crotch.

The three men laughed as they reviewed the scene that had just taken place in the dungeon.

"It is probably best if I act as protector," concluded Roebling.

It was agreed as the men continued to formulate a plan. The men had pulled out their cocks while continuing the conversation. All three were rubbing their shafts.

Wilhelm reappeared and was ordered to bring out Tomas and Thane, a boy the Commandants had not met.

"If you haven't noticed, Gentlemen, I have a slave for each day of the week. Tomas for Tuesdays, Wilhelm for Wednesdays, and Thane for tomorrow," von Wiedering explained.

"Do you rest on Sundays, Herr von Wiedering?" joked Roebling.

"I do, but my boy on Sunday certainly does not..."

Tomas, Wilhelm, and Thane soon appeared. A blonde, blue-eyed Aryan for each man. Naked, except for wrist restraints. They placed their hands behind their backs. Each boy knelt in front of one of the men. The sucking of German cock ensued.

All three men were aroused from the day's activities. Each was eager to fuck the face of the handsome Aryan in front of him. Roebling found Thane to have incredible sucking power and shot his German cumload first. Meissner was serviced by

Tomas and thrust his cock into the boy's thirsty throat before cumming with great force. Wilhelm knew how to please his Master and prolonged the pleasure. Finally, von Wiedering could hold it in no longer, and released his cumload into his slave's willing mouth.

The three boys lapped up the cum and then sat on their haunches, awaiting further instruction. They were dismissed.

von Wiedering ended the meeting by saying, "Well, Gentlemen, I think it is time the execution of your little play begins..." The two Commandants adjourned to the basement.

von Wiedering wanted to think and so, remained on the terrace, formulating plans of his own.

"An American boy in my stable would be a real asset," he mused, "I could probably sell the boy a dozen times or more. What German aristocrat wouldn't like to fuck an American whenever he wants to?" As he continued to smoke his cigar, he rationalized, "And what rich American wouldn't like a German officer to fuck?" In his mind, he viewed Meissner and Roebling chained to a wall. "Hmmm, within the realm of possibility?"

The American's head lolled to one side and his body hung limply, supported by his wrists in the manacles.

"Stand at attention, boy. Your Commandants are here!" yelled Meissner.

The boy attempted to stand at attention, but his knees buckled and he slumped back down. He had not been fed for several days nor given anything to drink.

Meissner slapped him across the face. "You have disobeyed your Commandant," yelled Meissner. He smacked the American's chest with his riding crop and began a more focused beating on the American's cock and balls.

The American groaned but did not struggle.

"Commandant, the American has taken our punishment well. If he weren't serious about working with us, he would not have tried to stand at attention in his weakened state," pleaded Roebling in a most convincing voice.

"He is a lying swine and needs to be punished..." Meissner flatly stated. The two staged an argument for the benefit of the prisoner. The arguing accelerated, riding crops were drawn.

Meissner yelled, "Fuck you! Der Fuehrer commissioned us to find out the truth. He will be interested to hear of your impotency in this endeavor..."

"As Senior Commandant, you may leave, Meissner, while I interrogate the prisoner in my own way," said Roebling with authority in his voice.

"Fuck you!" Meissner retorted as he marched out of the dungeon, his heels clicking on the basement floor.

"Well, Herr Franz, it's now just you and me. And I have the authority to loosen your manacles." He had secured the key from the ring of keys near the dungeon door.

He unlocked the cuffs. The American slumped. The Nazi supported his body and escorted him to a rustic armed chair.

Roebling pulled the bell cord in the dungeon and Wilhelm soon appeared.

"Yes, Sir? How may I be of service to you, Sir?"

"Our prisoner has not been fed since he arrived. Can you get him some food and something to drink, Wilhelm?"

"Jawohl, Mein Commandant."

Roebling turned his attention to Franz.

"How old are you, son?"

"Twenty-seven... Sir." Franz remembered his severe punishment when he did not address Commandant Meissner as 'Sir'.

"And how long have you been in the United States Military?"

"Ten years... Sir. I enlisted the day after I graduated from high school."

"So, you rose through the ranks very quickly to become one of the inner circle..." Roebling continued, in a kindly, almost fatherly voice. He rested his gloved hand on the boy's aching shoulder. He began massaging the boy's back which was crusted in blood. The American emitted a slight sigh, "Oh, thank you, Sir, that feels so good..."

Wilhelm appeared with a heaping plate of roast beef, boiled eggs, boiled potatoes, and bread. A pitcher of beer and two glasses were also on the tray. The American devoured the plate of food within a few moments. He drank three glasses of beer. He thanked Roebling several times.

"I'm sure, Herr Franz, that you will feel refreshed if you can sleep the night. And then, we can reconvene. I'm sure that you will be more cooperative at that point."

The American did not reply, savoring the taste of food, real food.

While Roebling was playing confidante to Franz, Meissner returned to his bedroom, thinking his performance brilliant. The American would reveal all. Der Fuehrer would be pleased and Meissner's family would be redeemed. Meissner was restless, however, and began wandering randomly through the extensive house. As he was an assertive, and an arrogant member of the SS Party, he did not ask – he took. Thus, he did not seek permission from Herr von Wiedering, he simply took it for granted that what was von Wiedering's was also available to his guest, Commandant Meissner.

Door after door was opened, revealing bedrooms, sitting rooms, rooms filled with paintings waiting to be hung. As he opened yet another door, he viewed a large bed, similar to the one in his room. Unlike the one in his room, however, this bed contained a naked youth. His arms and legs were tied to the four corners of the bed.

Meissner quickly closed the door and sauntered over to the bed.

"Well, well, well, Herr von Wiedering certainly has his week of boys lined up."

The boy was aware of Meissner's presence, but could not reply – a gag was in his mouth.

Meissner removed the gag and ordered the young man to reveal his name.

The young man did not immediately respond. Meissner slapped him across the cheek with his riding crop.

"Answer me, boy."

"I am Frederik."

"Ah, let me guess, Herr von Wiedering's Friday boyslave."

"You are correct, Sir."

"Does he keep you tied up when it is not your day of service?"

"Nein, Mein Commandant, I am being disciplined."

"For what, boy?" demanded the Nazi.

"I was sent to retrieve an ashtray before the ashes on his cigar dropped. I did not retrieve it quickly enough and his ash fell on the carpet, burning a hole."

The Nazi rubbed his riding crop across the boy's handsome ass.

"Well, boy, burning a hole is a serious misdemeanor. You should be disciplined for such an infraction."

Meissner's cock had started to rise with this last statement.

"Holes need to be filled, boy."

The boy did not answer. Meissner didn't really care to hear any answer as his sadistic cock tented his breeches even further. He marched to the head of the bed and shoved the gag back in the boy's mouth.

He unbuttoned his breeches and straddled the boy's naked ass.

He rubbed his lengthening shaft and added a little spittle for lubrication.

His cock eased up the boy's fuckhole. The boy struggled but it was useless.

The German cock crawled further up the boy's rectum as Meissner stretched his Leathered body on top of the naked boy.

He began slowly pumping his German rod further and further into the young man. The boy groaned, but apparently was a veteran of such action.

The Nazi began rubbing his Leathered body against the Aryan body. Rubbing his arms, his shoulders, reaching around and pulling on the boy's nips.

The boy was responding with moans. His asscheeks expanded and contracted as the German meat imbedded itself in his hole.

Pumping slowly and evenly, then more forcibly. The German's sweat dripped from his forehead onto the boy's back.

The boy's ass began to move in rhythm with the German's pumping.

Meissner prolonged the action as long as he could. He reared up once or twice, with cock intact, to flog the boy's back with his riding crop. The boy arched his shoulder blades so that he could feel the full force of the riding crop.

Meissner pulled the boy's head back savagely, holding his gloved hand over the gagged mouth. The boy was enjoying it – Meissner could tell. And so was he.

He pumped harder and harder, slapping the boy's cheeks with his riding crop. Pulling on the boy's tits. Leather against the boy's naked skin. Both were now sweating and their sweat intermingled.

Meissner's booted feet gripped the calves of the boy as his cock pumped harder and harder.

One final thrust and Meissner spilled his seed inside the boy's ass. The boy and Meissner both shuddered from the forced delivery of jism.

Meissner momentarily collapsed on top of the boy.

Ten minutes elapsed before Meissner revived. Pulling himself off of the boy, he crawled off the bed and readjusted his breeches.

He marched to the front of the bed and announced, "Not a bad fuck, Frederik. If you were my boy, you would certainly be fucked more than once a week..."

The boy did not reply – simply lay there, panting.

Meissner left the room.

CHAPTER SEVEN

A Deal, Struck in Leather

The American had been escorted to a room where he was allowed the luxury of a hot bath under the watchful eyes of the Nazi guards who had accompanied him and stood outside. It felt so good to erase the filth and dried blood. His aching body relished the feel of the hot, soapy water.

He prolonged the bath as long as he could. God knows what would happen to him next.

While in the tub, he thought of all that had happened. His mind came back time and again to Commandant Meissner. "My God! He is so damned attractive. I'd say anything to win his favor. I meant it when I said I wanted to be his fuckslave. Those steel blue eyes and his handsome, muscular body. That beautiful tight Leather covering every inch of his ass," Fritz thought as he sunk down into the tub, his soaped-up hand pulling on his lengthening cock. "And the tight gloves caressing his hands. His powerful lashes against my back. Taking his fucking manrod up my ass. Fuck! In another time and place, I would somehow overpower him and have my way with him. Take him into the woods, tie him to a tree, and work his ass over like he has done to me." The American closed his eyes and fantasized the whole episode. Two equally, masculine men, in another time and place. Bodies colliding. Kissing. Sucking. Fucking. Savagely whipping each other and then crawling under the sheets of their bed and making love. His dick was rock hard. He stroked it with his soaped-up hands. He pulled on it harder and harder, fantasizing that Meissner would crawl into the tub and suck him underneath the bath water.

That image of Meissner's mouth encircling his hardened cock hastened him toward ejaculation. A geyser of jism shot straight up out of the water. Some of the jism fell on his chin and cheeks and he hastily lapped it up.

Not long after, the guards came in, unannounced.

"All right, Prisoner. Enough time. We already know you wanked off – we heard you," one of the guards taunted. "Dry yourself off. We have orders to escort you to a room. Don't get any fucking ideas about escape. Your room has no windows. And we will be standing guard all night." They both laughed heartily as they viewed the American's cock which had shrunk back to normal size.

The room was richly appointed, with a huge four-postered bed with heavy bedcurtains to keep away the night drafts. He sunk into the soft mattress and pillows. It didn't take him long to fall asleep.

Franz was not sure how long he had been asleep, but a hand was shaking him. A gloved hand was over his mouth. The room, with no windows, was pitch black. Franz couldn't see six inches in front of him.

A German voice whispered hoarsely, "Just listen. Don't talk. I can get you out of here. The Germans have no plans to use you as a confidante. They are escorting you back to Der Fuehrer, so that he can personally torture you until death. They don't believe you have any secrets to share. They are tiring of your firm resolve not to talk. I will give you one hour to decide."

"Wait..." Franz started in a loud voice.

The voice reappeared at his side, "You want the Guards in here, you ignorant swine? I'll return in one hour."

Despite squinting into the darkness and straining his ears to hear any sound, the American could hear no footsteps retreating.

"What to do?" the American wondered. If he stayed, he would undoubtedly be killed. If he tried to run, he would certainly be killed – the Guards who stood outside his door had not been beaten and tortured like he had been over the past several days. Even though he had just enjoyed a bath and solid food, he was still no match for the Guards. He could never overpower one, let alone two. It seemed to him that the only logical tact to take was to follow the German 'voice'. "But, wait," he thought to himself, "how did the German get in the room – did the Guards let him in? There were no windows. Could there be a secret passage – how in the hell can I find it in pitch darkness?" He moved around the room as stealthily as possible, pushing on moldings, twisting knobs on cupboards, but to no avail. "It's futile, I'll never get out of this situation alive." He crawled back into the bed. From sheer exhaustion, he fell into a fitful sleep. He dreamed that he was being carried from the inescapable room by an unknown person.

Except it wasn't a dream. Two hooded men had entered the room from a secret passageway and had secreted the prisoner into a private dungeon room. He was manacled to a rough, wooden table and left. The two hooded men re-entered the bedchamber and stole across the room. Turning the doorknob ever so slowly, they yanked the door open and fell on the two guards. Caught by surprise, the guards were no match for the hooded men who quickly subdued them with rags soaked in chloroform over their mouth and nostrils. Leaving the door wide open, the guards were dragged away, taken to secret chambers within the house.

The hooded men evaporated into the darkness of the night.

As the sun peaked over the horizon, a furious banging was heard first on the door of Roebling's room, and then on the door of Meissner's room.

The two Nazis rushed out of bed to see what the commotion was all about. It was Herr von Wiedering in a state of undress and clearly upset.

"The prisoner and the Guards – they are GONE!"

"What the fuck?" Roebling replied. Both Nazis pulled on their breeches and followed von Wiedering down the hall to the room where Franz was taken. It was true – he had vanished. The Nazi guards were not to be seen either. von Wiedering pulled the bellpull and his bevy of naked boyslaves came rushing. They were naked except for their wrist restraints.

von Wiedering lined them against the wall. He had retrieved his heavy Leather flogger.

"Our American prisoner has escaped with the two guards. If any of you helped them, you will be flogged until you are without skin on your ass, I assure you."

One by one, the naked, trembling boys were questioned by von Wiedering, by Meissner, and by Roebling. If one of them hesitated in his answer, he was lashed by one of the Leathermen.

"Herr von Wiedering, I suggest we take all seven into the dungeon and chain them up until one confesses."

He ordered his boys down to the dungeon.

The Nazis retrieved their riding crops from their rooms and hastened downstairs. The boys were all chained tightly to the dungeon walls. Each was scrutinized by each of the Nazis. Two hours later, not one had confessed.

"Gentlemen, let us convene upstairs." suggested von Wiedering. He released Thane and ordered him to bring coffee to the east terrace.

The Commandants and their host sat out on the terrace. Coffee was brought by Thane.

He kneeled in front of his Master. "Sirs, please believe me, I had nothing to do with this."

"You fucking better not have had anything to do with this, asshole," Roebling angrily hissed and struck him across the cheek, "The American prisoner is the property of Der Fuehrer and anyone who aided and abetted the prisoner will be put to death." The boy trembled.

"Herr von Wiedering, as Commandant, I want every inch of this compound searched," Roebling ordered. "The prisoner must be found. In the interim, Der Fuehrer will know nothing of this. We must convey a communication, however, to Der Fuehrer that we have been delayed in our mission and must remain here until all is accomplished."

"Jawohl, Commandant Roebling. I will gladly assist in the search. The only others on the compound are my boyslaves. We will have to enlist their aid as well," von Wiedering answered as a generous smile met the Nazis' eyes.

"Nein, they will be left as is until we resolve the matter."

"As you wish, Commandant Roebling."

The Nazis returned to their respective bedrooms to dress in their Leather uniforms.

"Roebling, I'm going to search the north corridor where the American's room is," Meissner stated as he marched out of the room. He had a hunch.

He entered the room and closed the door behind him. He began examining every inch of molding along the baseboard, the fireplace surround, the back of the fireplace.

"These old houses often have secret passageways...," he thought to himself.

As he stood on the hearth of the fireplace, he noted that one of the bricks was loose. He wiggled it with his booted foot. He pried it up and there was a cylindrical knob embedded in the floor. He turned it and a portion of the paneling cracked open. Meissner quickly exited into the narrow passageway, following a number of pitch black tunnels. After retracing his steps several times from dead ends, he came upon a small chamber. Wooden table. Meissner could just make out a human form on top of it.

"Franz, is that you? It's Commandant Meissner. Answer me, who brought you here?"

"It's Franz, Sir. Sir, I have no idea – it was all done in complete darkness."

"I've got to get you back to Der Fuehrer."

"No, Sir, please don't, they will kill me."

"What makes you think that?"

"I'm not useful. I won't reveal my secrets. I only said that I wanted to defect to curry favor with you. I find you... attractive."

Meissner chortled, "What the fuck, prisoner? I am your sworn enemy, you asshole."

"I meant it when I said I wanted to be your fuckslave. I want to take your cock up my ass and down my throat. I want to lick your cock and lick your boots and be flogged by you every day, Sir."

"I have to admit, Franz, that you have taken more punishment than any other interrogation candidate I have ever worked over. You are a very strong man and I admire that. Of all the asses I have fucked, I enjoyed fucking you because I know you enjoyed it and took it like a man. Not like my Father, who was weak. In another place and time, things might have been different. But you are Der Fuehrer's property and to take you into my personal possession would be professional suicide."

"Still," the Nazi mused silently, "I would enjoy coming home to this boy's willing ass every day. Take all my aggressions out on his willing body. Flogging. Fucking. Fisting," the Nazi began to moan as his dick stirred in his Leather breeches, "I am of the Aryan nation. I take what I want."

He quickly crawled on top of the manacled American. Unleashing his extended dick from his pants, he guided it toward the American's mouth. Franz swallowed the German cock and began a spirited sucking on it. The German was panting as he took Franz's cock in his mouth. Franz's cock began to swell with the Commandant's licking and sucking.

Their sex was hurried and savage. Cumjuice soon spilled from both men's dicks and it was lapped up by what could have been misconstrued as two hungry dogs.

Fortunately, the manacles were tied into place and not locked. Meissner untied the ropes and escorted Franz out of the room. He led him through the passageways, stole down the hallway and secreted him in his own room. "Who would think of looking here?" he thought. He tied the prisoner to the bedpost with some lengths of Leather he always carried. To the viewer, the boy could not be seen – he was hidden behind the bedcurtains. "I will return when it is safe."

The American leaned forward and kissed Meissner on the cheek, "Thank you, Mein Commandant." Meissner left, rubbing the cheek as if he had been slapped.

As he exited his room, Roebling was striding toward him. "Where the fuck have you been – taking a nap, Meissner?"

"Nein, Roebling. Merely taking a much-needed crap."

"Well, get on with it. The prisoner must be found. Or we will pay dearly for it."

"Fuck Der Fuehrer," Meissner thought, "My desires come first."

CHAPTER 8

The Recapture

Roebling was furious. He stalked the halls like a crazed man. Pushing doors open, knocking furniture aside. The prisoner and the two missing guards had to be secreted within the compound. And he was going to find out who took them.

He marched down the grand staircase, his booted heels clicking on the marble steps. He found von Wiedering and his boyslave Thane preparing the dining table for lunch.

"Herr von Wiedering, I wish to speak to you in private," Roebling commanded.

"Yes, Commandant, what is it you wish to speak to me about?"

"Hiding war criminals is of the highest treason against Der Fuehrer, and I am certain you know more about this than you are telling us..."

"Commandant, why would I jeopardize not only my friendship with Der Fuehrer, but jeopardize my life here," the host calmly replied as he rearranged the place settings on the table.

"Accompany me to the dungeon, Herr von Wiedering, NOW!"

von Wiedering followed Roebling down to the dungeon where his six boyslaves were still manacled to the wall. Without warning, Roebling wrenched the man's hands behind his back and manacled him into the seventh position.

"Commandant, this is outrageous. Release me immediately, or I will have Der Fuehrer demote you and send you off on a train to one of the camps."

"Shut the fuck up, von Wiedering. I am in command," Roebling replied as he savagely lashed the man's face. He drew blood.

"You fucking bastard," von Wiedering cried as his boyslave rushed to his side.

"You, boy, get over there... stay out of this." Roebling replied. Thane obeyed the Commandant and retreated to the other side of the room.

Meissner marched down into the basement. "Roebling, have you lost your mind? He is our host..."

"He is a traitor and he will tell us where he hid the American and the guards."

Roebling proceeded to slap the host repeatedly across the face. He pulled out the man's cock and balls and squeezed with an iron grip. von Wiedering winced in pain. "Roebling," he gasped, "you are making a fundamental mistake!"

"No, Herr, you made the mistake. You took that American and I have a suspicion that you are going to sell him into the slave trade. Correct me if I am wrong, Herr," Roebling pronounced as he tightened the grip on the man's cock and balls.

"All right, all right, I did take him. It was stupid of me. But we can make a profit. We can divide the money."

"You won't have a pot to piss in when I'm through with you, Herr von Wiedering."

Meissner stood silently by.

"You will take us immediately to the guards and then the American, NOW! Meissner grab his left arm."

von Wiedering was accompanied upstairs, guarded by the two Nazis. He led them upstairs and through a passageway into a secret chamber where the two guards were blindfolded and gagged. They were tightly lashed to the wall and it took some time to untie them. When released, the guards took charge of the new prisoner. Reluctantly he led them through the dark tunnels to the room where he had secreted the American prisoner.

"Here is the room," von Wiedering proclaimed as he led the way into the secret portion of the compound. His jaw dropped open as it was revealed that the table was empty.

"You fucking liar," Roebling yelled as he kicked the prisoner with his booted foot. His knee punched von Wiedering's crotch and the man doubled over in pain.

"I swear to you this is where we placed him. He has somehow escaped." von Wiedering was sweating profusely. Roebling let loose with a barrage of whippings with his riding crop, catching the man's back and chest.

"Liar. Tell us the truth, you lying piece of shit. Guards, escort him to his dungeon. Meissner, oversee his interrogation. I want the truth and we will have it."

von Wiedering was escorted back to the dungeon and was spread-eagled on a table of his own devising. He was placed face down. He was shaking his head, pleading with his eyes. "Meissner, I swear to you. I left the American tied up in the room we just left."

"Shut the fuck up, asshole. You are lying. We will loosen your tongue," Meissner replied, the steel blue glint returning to his eyes. He knew the truth, but he was going to prolong the torture to satisfy his own sadistic desires. He retrieved a black Leather hood from a nearby shelf and placed it over von Wiedering's head. He roughly stuffed a rag in von Wiedering's mouth.

His cock arched in his breeches as he knew what he was going to do next. He pulled it out and massaged it into fullness.

He spread von Wiedering's asscheeks and plunged his German rod into the receptive hole.

von Wiedering's screams could be heard upstairs. "Good," thought Roebling, "he will confess."

Meissner plunged his cock in and out of the fuckhole. This form of interrogation was his favorite activity as he flogged the man's back with his riding crop.

"Herr von Wiedering, you have been a naughty boy and you must be punished. My cock is enjoying your hole as it reaches further and further into your rectum."

The man was screaming into the rag that plugged his mouth. It just made Meissner pump harder and harder, faster and faster. His Leathered legs slapping against the edge of the table. Meissner was gripping the man's asscheeks with an iron grip, spreading them further and further apart as his rod drilled deeper and deeper.

Meissner was sweating. He began slapping von Wiedering's asscheeks as his cock swelled to full-size.

The man continued to scream as Meissner thrust the last inch of his shaft up the man's ass. A mighty sea of jism exploded in the man's asshole. He screamed and Meissner screamed, "FUCK!" as his manjuices lubricated the asshole of the traitor.

Meissner continued to thrust his cock in and out, now fully coated with his own semen.

After what seemed an eternity, he withdrew. The man on the table was heaving.

Meissner marched around to the front of the table. Leaning down, he looked into von Wiedering's eyes, and said, "I have a little confession of my own, Herr, I know where the American is." With that he spit in the man's hooded face and laughed, "I just wanted to fuck you. We will make a deal. You say nothing to Roebling and I will get you out of this mess you are in. Agreed?"

The man did not have much choice but to agree to whatever Meissner was going to propose.

Meanwhile, Roebling was storming around upstairs, ripping down curtains, looking under beds, thundering around, cursing.

"Remain here, Herr. I will take care of it." He laughed sadistically as he said this, as, of course, there was no way that von Wiedering could escape his own dungeon.

Meissner climbed to the first floor, on the lookout for Roebling. He calmly ascended the staircase to the second floor and entering his room, untied the American from his bedpost, retied his hands behind him and went in search of Roebling. He warned the American not to say anything to Roebling.

He eventually found Roebling in an outbuilding, searching through packing trunks.

"Mein Commandant, von Wiedering has confessed and the American has been found," Meissner calmly stated.

"What?" Roebling said. He was so intense in his search that he had not heard Meissner and Franz enter the building.

"I received a confession from von Wiedering and here is the American." The American stood calmly by Meissner's side.

Roebling sighed a sigh of relief. "Where was he?"

"Herr von Wiedering simply had the wrong room. There are many hidden rooms within the compound. As you suggested, he wanted the boy for his own. To train. To sell. Greed took over when he saw a handsome young man. Roebling, in that sense, you can't blame him – the prisoner is handsome...for an American."

"I'll personally string up von Wiedering by his balls and let him twist in the wind... the fucking bastard."

"He wishes to apologize for his transgression, Roebling. I gave him an assfucking that he won't soon forget."

This last statement seemed to calm Roebling for the moment.

"We need to pack up and take the prisoner back to Der Fuehrer. I'll make a full report and Der Fuehrer can deal with von Wiedering."

"Now, Roebling, if we tell Der Fuehrer of this escapade, who do you think will be blamed? Us. We were in charge of the prisoner and we were duped. Who do you think will be blamed? Us. I suggest we pack up and leave and not mention it to anyone."

CHAPTER NINE

American Boyslave

Hours later, the Nazi officers returned to Der Fuehrer's headquarters in Berlin with their American prisoner and the two guards. The two guards were instructed to say nothing about their hours in captivity. Although each one of them wanted to beat the hell out of von Wiedering, they were sternly ordered to remain silent.

"Sieg Heil," they both shouted as Der Fuehrer entered his office, emblazoned with the SS symbol prominently displayed on the flag behind his desk.

"Sit, Mein Commandants," he ordered.

A handsome young Nazi officer, obviously proud to be Der Fuehrer's aide, presented them with drinks and a selection of cigars from Der Fuehrer's walnut humidor.

They gave a full report of their activities, omitting the kidnapping escapade carried out by von Wiedering. For the moment, he would get away with it. Roebling and Meissner discussed retribution before their conference with Der Fuehrer.

The news was not good – bombing missions had increased and the Allied Forces had gained ground.

Der Fuehrer pronounced his plan. "I am convinced after your review that the American is worthless to us. If he had wanted to be useful to us, he would have given us the secrets he holds in his pathetic, useless mind. Therefore, Meissner, I want you to personally see that he is executed by this afternoon. Make sure he is never found. I don't need to know the details. Carry it out swiftly."

"Jawohl, Der Fuehrer," Meissner replied. A seed of doubt was already swirling around in his head, but to disobey Der Fuehrer's direct order would be treason. He would be stripped of his duties and he himself would probably be sent on the trains.

They were dismissed. Der Fuehrer had more pressing details with which to deal.

As they walked out of the headquarters, Roebling turned to Meissner, "How are we going to execute that worthless piece of American shit?"

"Commandant, since I have such a strong personal distaste for him, I will carry it out myself. I think one final assfuck and then I slit his throat while he is still spread-eagled on my table."

Roebling smiled a sadistic smile and replied, "I trained you well. Let's rendezvous tomorrow. I want to hear details."

A sedan for each Nazi was awaiting their departure. Meissner entered the sedan with his American prisoner, tightly bound and blindfolded. Meissner returned to Ravensbrueck and without briefing his staff, retreated to his office. He personally escorted the prisoner into his office. He propped his feet up on the desk, thinking his plan through. The Aryan boy that he had not been able to take on his ordered detail knocked on the door, and entered when instructed to do so.

"Commandant, what a pleasure to see you," Hans Buchner said as he beamed from ear to ear.

"Find me a drink, boy. My cigars are missing – find a Cuban cigar for me as well." The boy hastened out of the office.

The boy had hoped that he would be ordered to crawl between his Commandant's legs but that was not the case – yet.

The Commandant began to write an order which he would hand Buchner as soon as he returned. It ordered the execution of one prisoner who had recently been returned to incarceration. A physical description was given for ease of identification.

The boy returned with the cigar, clipped, and a bottle of brandy with a snifter.

"What else might I do for you, Commandant?" the young Aryan said, hopeful that it would include a cock-sucking of the Commandant's cock.

"Take this order to Bilinkoff immediately."

"Jawohl, Mein Commandant. Nothing else, Sir?"

"Nein, be on your way...." as he dismissed the boy with a wave of his hand.

The Commandant rose from his chair and locked the office door. He pulled the American officer from underneath his desk.

He untied the soldier. In gratitude, Franz kissed the officer on the cheek, saying "Thank you, Mein Commandant."

He slapped the prisoner sharply across the cheek. "You will do as I tell you. This is a risk. Disobey and I will slit your throat."

He ordered the soldier back under the desk as he unbuttoned his breeches and pulled out his cock. The soldier needed no instruction in the sucking of the Commandant's throbbing rod. As he smoked his cigar, he pulled the boy's head toward his crotch until the soldier's mouth was fully engulfed with the German cock. It did not take Meissner long to climax. He was resettling his cock in his breeches when a knock sounded on the door.

The Commandant ordered the boy to be as silent as possible as he headed toward the door.

"Sieg Heil, Mein Commandant," saluted Bilinkoff.

The Commandant returned his salute and ushered Bilinkoff to the other end of the office.

"Is there a problem, Bilinkoff?"

"Commandant, you neglected to put in the prisoner's name. We have several who were sent for incarceration who fit the description. Three to be exact"

Meissner stammered for only a second before ordering the execution of all three. "Bilinkoff, I want them to disappear. Not a trace. Am I understood?" The steel blue glint in his eyes pierced Bilinkoff's questioning eyes, erasing the possibility of any questions.

"I will fill out the necessary paperwork." as he dismissed Bilinkoff.

He exited the office with Bilinkoff and headed to a storeroom. Several minutes later, he returned to his office with a pair of boots, breeches, jacket, and Muir cap.

He once again re-entered his office and the American quickly dressed in a Nazi uniform. It wasn't a perfect fit, but it would have to do. And in the cover of darkness, the guards would hopefully not notice the discrepancy. The boots were much too small as Franz struggled to put them on.

"Let me look at you," Meissner ordered.

The jacket was tightly buttoned over Meissner's muscular chest. Meissner hoped that the American could walk to the sedan without tripping or falling in the tight boots.

At 0200 hours, Meissner and his aide exited the office. The guards at the front entrance snapped to attention when Commandant Meissner appeared. "I am heading to my apartment for the evening. Which sedan is available?"

"I will retrieve it for you, Mein Commandant." Franz stood behind Meissner and avoided eye contact with either guard.

The other sentry looked at Franz, partially hidden from view. "You don't look familiar to me, soldier."

Meissner interceded before Franz could say a word, "This is the nephew of an old friend of mine. Recently entered Der

Fuehrer's Army. I told my friend I would take care of him while he is on detachment from headquarters in Austria."

"Looks like you could use a new uniform. Your armband is missing. Der Fuehrer would be very displeased."

Without raising his head, Franz replied, "Jawohl. I'll see to it immediately." He had been incarcerated long enough, listening to Meissner and Roebling often enough, to effect a passable German accent.

The sedan pulled up and Meissner hastened Franz into the passenger side. Meissner climbed into the driver's seat and sped off into the night.

Meissner maintained a small apartment an hour away from the compound and he hoped that there would be no blockades.

The guards stood watching them depart.

"Hmm, the Commandant seemed a little too anxious to impart details about that soldier..."

"Fuck, it's another one of the Commandant's whores, no doubt."

Their conversation would have probably continued but just then, the front door opened and Bilinkoff brought out three prisoners. They were tightly bound and blindfolded. Two guards escorted them.

"Three prisoners. Commandant's orders are forthcoming. Need I say more?"

"Nein, Bilinkoff."

Not long after, several shots rang out and a bonfire was viewed from a distance. The compound then settled down for the night.

Meissner drove slowly to his destination. The prisoner remained silent on the drive.

They arrived at Meissner's apartment. Looking left to right, behind him and in front of him, Meissner escorted the American into his apartment.

He locked the door.

"Well, Franz, how does it feel to be a member of the SS?"

"It feels fucking wonderful, Sir." He once again kissed Meissner, but this time of the lips. Meissner recoiled.

He slapped Franz across the cheek. "I am a SS officer and did not bring you here for such unwelcome sentimentality. You are here as my fuckslave and you will remain so." He grabbed the neck of the American and escorted him roughly to the bedroom. The bedroom was spare. A bed and a bureau. A generous, full-length mirror. The Nazi flag was tacked over the bed as a makeshift headboard.

Meissner pushed Franz on the bed as he tugged at his Leather breeches. His cock swelled as his breeches were lowered around his knees. Straddling the boy's legs, Meissner tugged at the boy's breeches. The boy's handsome naked ass made Meissner's cock rise even more.

Meissner fell on top of Franz and plugged the boy's hole with his swollen cock. The invasion was quick and violent and both men enjoyed it.

"Fuck me, Mein Commandant!" the boy moaned. "I have waited for this, fuck me. Fuck me harder."

Meissner pumped his cock harder and harder into the willing hole. He soon climaxed. His Leather uniformed body collapsed on top of the boy and they lay there silently for some time. Franz was relishing every minute spent with this powerful man.

Meissner finally climbed off the boy. The boy rolled over – a smile of ecstasy on his face.

"Mein Commandant, that was perfect. But, please, Sir, I want to taste your mouth on my lips," the boy pleaded.

"Nein," the Commandant answered. He once again slapped the boy across the cheek, "Remove the uniform and take a shower."

Franz had difficulty removing the tight boots, but finally headed into the shower. As he soaped himself, he played with his cock. It hardened very quickly as he thought of his new situation. He was in the private apartment of Meissner – a high-profile member of the SS. He had felt the power of the man when the man's cock thrust into his asshole and the power of his cum when his officer's cock shot a load up his ass. He wanted to taste that cock in his mouth, taste the cum on his lips. His dick was throbbing, pulsating up and down when the shower curtain was pulled back. The Commandant was naked and entered the shower.

Franz started to embrace the Commandant but was pushed away.

"Down on your knees, boy."

Franz fell to his knees and that throbbing cock was inserted in his willing mouth.

The Commandant soaped himself absently as his cock pushed in and pulled out of the slave's mouth.

Franz closed his eyes and continued the vacuuming of his Master's cock. He tenderly reached up and caressed the man's low-hanging balls. He looked up, only to find that the Commandant had his eyes closed as well. Franz eased off and gave the man a well-deserved suck massage of his member. The water from the shower was pulsating against the naked bodies of the two men. Franz wanted to lick every inch of the man's masculine body. He wanted to stick his tongue in the man's asshole. Tongue his nipples. The fur-line extending from his chest to his cock. His muscular arms.

Meissner increased the pressure on the boy's head so that his mouth was fully engorged on Meissner's cock. They continued for some time until Meissner began moaning. Franz knew that climax was near and began a more vigorous cocksucking. Ribbons of jism coursed down his throat as Meissner's back arched and his hands became iron vises around Franz's head.

Meissner stood silently for some time before releasing the boy's head.

"Good boy," he said, as he exited the shower and toweled himself dry. The two men slept soundly. The Nazi's arm wrapped protectively around the boy's shoulder.

CHAPTER TEN

Plans Made in Leather

Meissner had always been an early riser and the next morning was no exception.

As the sun peaked over the horizon, Meissner was up. He slapped the boy on the ass and instructed him to get out of bed. Each had only gotten two or three hours of sleep after the rigors of the previous day.

"Ass out of bed, boy. Your Master needs your attention. Fix coffee for me. You'll find what you need in the kitchen."

The boy shuffled to the kitchen, still half asleep. As he placed the coffee in the percolator, he realized that he had spent his first night with his German Master. It energized him and he hastened the preparations. His LeatherMaster had already pulled on his Leather breeches and spitshined boots. He was seated in the living area of the apartment.

While the coffee percolated, the boy came into the living area and knelt at his Master's feet. He began licking the man's boots, using his chest to massage the calves of the boots.

"That's right, boy. Get them polished." He was swatted with the Leatherman's bare hand when he missed a spot.

The boy wanted his Master to look the best of the Nazi officers in the compound.

When the coffee was ready, he presented the cup to his Master and sat at his feet.

"Down on all fours, boy!"

The boy obliged and the Commandant rested his booted feet on his slave's back.

"I will be gone for most of the day. You are to remain here. Do not make noise. Do not peer out the windows." The windows were heavily curtained. "Under no circumstances are you to go outside. And do not answer a knock on the door. You will find a number of my boots in the hall closet. I want them all spitshined just like these."

After the officer had consumed two cups of coffee, he stood up and motioned for the boy to kneel beneath him.

"Open your mouth, slave." With that, Meissner pissed down the boy's throat, giving him his morning drink. The boy relished every drop.

"Help me dress, boy," Meissner instructed as he led the way to the bedroom. The man pulled on his Leather shirt, jacket, dress belt, and gloves. Tie tied precisely. His riding crop was tucked in the belt. Muir Cap firmly placed on his head, pulled low over the forehead.

"Do not forget what I told you or there will be hell to pay. And don't go back to bed. Clean this apartment," ordered Meissner.

"Jawohl, Mein Commandant," the boy meekly said. He would not forget his orders.

The Commandant left for a full day of activities. The War was heating up with the Allied forces gaining strength and victory on a daily basis. Der Fuehrer's War Cabinet was locked in daily sessions. Commandants of compounds were on full alert.

As Meissner arrived at the compound, a number of sedans were already in place. He marched into headquarters.

"Commandant, emergency meeting NOW!" announced one of the sentries.

The SS officers were briefed on all that had transpired. After two hours of continuous monologue and passed communiqués from Der Fuehrer, Meissner's mind began to wonder. He massaged the cock in his breeches, wishing that it were being serviced by the willing American.

During the course of the meeting, Karl Roebling marched in. He apologized for his lateness and sat in an empty chair behind Meissner.

During a brief lull between reports, Roebling leaned over the Meissner and hoarsely whispered, "Is the problem eradicated, Commandant?"

Answering in the affirmative, Meissner drew his index finger across his throat.

"Good work, I trained you well." Meissner felt a twinge of guilt at deceiving Roebling, but it was quickly suppressed, thinking, "I am of the Aryan nation. I take what I want."

The meeting lasted until well into the afternoon. Prisoners were to be deported as quickly as the trains could be loaded. Out of this area into more remote areas. Commandants were to sign orders for executions as quickly as they received them.

Meissner returned to his office, only to find a shitload of paperwork. He tackled it after lighting a fresh Cuban – might as well enjoy a cigar while authorizing the extermination of the lesser classes. Nearly two hours passed before Meissner saw the top of his desk.

"What a fucking miserable way to spend the day!" he thought to himself. He had just lighted a fresh cigar and propped his feet on his desk when a knock sounded on his door.

As he pulled his boots off the desk, he yelled "Enter."

Roebling entered.

He sat in front of Meissner's desk.

"I have received a communication from our old friend von Wiedering...," Roebling began.

"Oh, and what did he have to say?" Meissner questioned.

"I'd rather not discuss it here. Thought I'd swing by your apartment after hours. What time?"

"No, can't do it," as Meissner re-lighted his cigar, trying to think up a valid excuse.

"Oh? Why? Some little German whoreboy sucking your cock?" Roebling taunted.

"No, Roebling, nothing like that. I've just got a lot to catch up on. We were at von Wiedering for only several days but the paperwork has increased tremendously. Hasn't yours?"

"Fuck, Meissner. This is an offer... from our friend."

"Not tonight," Meissner replied.

Roebling, who was quick to anger, rose from his chair and yelled "FUCK YOU!" in Meissner's face and stalked out.

"What the hell is wrong with Meissner?" He stalked out of the building.

"Get me transportation," he barked at one of the guards.

He paced back and forth, muttering to himself, "Fucking mutt. I trained him. Treat me like this – I should have whipped him."

"Mein Commandant, is there a problem?"

"Oh, it's just Meissner. Acts like he has a pole up his ass."

"No, Sir, it was more likely that he stuck his pole up an ass last night," the guard replied.

"Explain your statement, soldier."

The guard filled him in, adding his suspicions that the young Nazi in the ill-fitting outfit was not the nephew of an old friend. Roebling thanked the guard for the information.

"So, I was right when I said that Meissner is keeping a whore for himself. I may pay Meissner a visit tonight," he thought to himself.

The sedan arrived and Roebling drove away.

Meissner continued to work on new directives which arrived shortly after Roebling stormed out of the office, but he finally left at 2100 hours. As he drove to his apartment, he massaged his cock. He looked forward to fucking his slave's willing ass. The apartment was dark as ordered. He unlocked the door and flipped on the nearest light. He closed and locked the door.

The naked boy was kneeling in the living area. He viewed his spitshined boots, neatly lined against the wall in the bedroom.

"Good evening, Mein Commandant. I have prepared you something to eat. I know you must be hungry."

The man cuffed the boy's head and replied "Good boy."

He headed to the living area and ate the meal without comment. His appetite was only satisfied in one area. A nice long fuck session would relax him. He ordered the boy into the bedroom. The boy lay spread-eagled on the freshly-made bed.

Meissner stood looking at the boy, massaging his Leathered crotch.

A hard pounding on the door interrupted his action of unbuttoning his breeches.

"Quick, boy, crawl in here," the Commandant ordered. The bureau had a false front, disguised as drawers. It led to a secret cavity in the wall hollowed out by Meissner for the storage of contraband – his treasured Cuban cigars for instance. The boy barely fit. Meissner's mind was quick as he threw in the boy's discarded uniform as well.

As a second more insistent pounding on the door was heard, Meissner closed the cabinet front. He marched to the door and jerked it open.

"Roebling, what the hell do you want?"

"I told you I wanted to talk to you."

"And you don't listen very well, I said tonight was not convenient."

"Herr Meissner, I will tell you when I take orders from you. I trained you and I can ruin you."

The two Nazis glowered at each other. Roebling entered the living area, "Well, I see you have already eaten. How about offering your guest a glass of wine?"

Meissner selected a wine glass from the cupboard and poured Roebling a glass of red wine from the opened bottle on the table.

Roebling made himself comfortable on the sofa. His eyes scanned Meissner's stony face for a transgression of expression.

"The guard tells me that you escorted a young man to your vehicle last night."

Meissner was not surprised that the lout had revealed this to Roebling. "He will be appropriately punished," Meissner thought to himself.

"Yes, Roebling, that's correct. He was the nephew...," Meissner started.

"...of an old friend. Which old friend, Meissner?"

Dredging up a name from the past, Meissner quickly replied, "Werner. From our training camp days."

Roebling, fortunately for Meissner, did not have a recall of Werner.

Meissner elaborated, spinning the lie to greater proportions.

"So, where is this boy? I'd like to meet him."

"Ordered back to Austrian headquarters this morning."

"Are you sure, Meissner? He is not here?"

"Search if you'd like, Roebling. Frankly, I don't like your insinuations," stated Meissner, as he calmly sipped his glass of red wine. He poured himself some more.

"All right, Meissner. I guess I'm just over-reacting. In wartime, you suspect anyone and everyone of treason and traitorous acts. I should have known better. Not you – of all people. My apologies," Roebling finally remarked as he accepted a second glass of red wine. Meissner's face did not register any emotion, although he was feeling more guilt at deceiving Roebling.

After a long gulp of wine, Roebling continued "The matter at hand... I have received a letter from von Wiedering. It has profuse apologies for his behaviour. After our days with him, he realized that you and I have similar... proclivities, and he would like to see both of us eventually situated with one of his boys to aid us in our... interests. He would present them to each one of us as a token for not exposing his escapade to Der Fuehrer."

"Well, that is certainly a most generous offer...," Meissner was, for the moment, speechless, not knowing what to say.

"von Wiedering is talking of moving to South America, disbanding his operation here, and would like to see his boys relocated to suitable 'homes' before he leaves. He is offering us both positions as trainers for his stable of boys. He would like to increase it threefold. Think about it, Meissner. We'd be partners. Live the life that von Wiedering leads. Surrounded by handsome boys. Naked, at our beck and call. We could fuck them whenever we want. What say you, Meissner?"

"I must think about it. There is so much uncertainty, Roebling, you realize that. The Allied Forces are increasing their attacks and Der Fuehrer needs his Commandants more than ever."

"Meissner, the writing is on the wall. The Allied Forces are turning the tide. The Regime is beginning to crumble. If we stay until the bitter end, we might be tried as war criminals and end up like some of our victims. Der Fuehrer is beginning to loose his grip on reality. Didn't you hear the last speech? He sounded irrational. He's making hasty decisions based on bad counsel – his own and his inner circle. Not good ones. Again, what do you say, Meissner?

"I am... uncertain. Der Fuehrer may have had a momentary lapse in judgment. We stand to inherit the earth if we continue to support our great leader," Meissner said weakly.

"Have you gone mad, Meissner? Inherit the earth – shit! That was simply the rantings of an increasingly-demented leader. We'll wind up as rotting skin and bones in some prison for war criminals."

The conversation continued with no resolve. Meissner needed to digest all that had been said.

Roebling eventually changed the subject. Commenting on the excellent wine. He massaged his crotch. The rubbing motion was not lost on Meissner. The cock in his breeches was aroused at the sight of Roebling's black Leather glove rubbing on the boner in Roebling's breeches.

Seeing that Roebling had captured Meissner's attention, he remarked, "I thought you lived for the latest fuck," With that, Roebling reached over and grabbed Meissner's crotch area.

Soon, the two Leathermen were on the floor. In full uniform. In the sixty-nine position. Both had hold of the other's hard cock, being tongued by eager tongues, engulfed by lips.

Meissner pulled Roebling's cock out of his mouth briefly, to say, "Fuck, Roebling. I want your cock to choke me. It tastes so fucking good. The smell of your handsome Leather is on it."

Roebling simply nodded his head and continued sucking on Meissner's rod.

Their Leathered chests rubbing against each's abdomens. Booted feet flanking their heads. Their hands rubbing each other's thighs and calves which were encased in their tight, black Leather. The frenzied sucking continued. Tonguing the head, the shaft and the loose ballsac. Squeezing the shaft with their black Leather gloves. Gloves reaching into the breeches to squeeze the firm asscheeks. The pumping accelerated. The men were both pulling hard on each other's cocks with their mouths. Tongues were exploring the piss slit. The engorged head. The swollen shaft. Gloved hands were squeezing the ballsac.

The release of cum flooded each other's throats. They both licked their partner's cocks and excess of cum.

They lay in that position for some time.

Finally, Roebling extricated himself, straightened his uniform, repositioned his Muir cap, and said, "You will at least consider the proposal, Meissner."

Meissner agreed. He locked the door after Roebling's departure and rushed into the bedroom.

He unlocked the cabinet. The boy blinked and moaned. He had been in the same position for several hours.

Meissner began massaging the boy's arms and legs. They had fallen asleep. He picked the boy up and laid him on the bed.

"Thank you, Master. I would have stayed in there for a week if it would have made you happy," the boy said weakly.

Meissner retrieved a glass and poured some brandy into the glass for the boy to drink.

Slowly, the boy revived.

"Can you stand up, boy?" The boy slowly stood up. Meissner escorted him to the shower and turned the hot water spigot on. The boy was clinging to the side of the shower wall for a long time. His knees were still weakened.

Meissner undressed and joined the boy in the shower. He soaped the boy's back and reached around and soaped his chest. As he rotated his soapy hands toward the boy's privates, he felt the boy's cock. It was fully tumescent.

Meissner, who was not known for his humor, remarked, "Well, at least, boy, one part of you did not fall asleep."

"Master, I love you. You are so kind to me...," the boy started, but the man stopped him.

"I have purpose for soaping up your ass, boy. I want to fuck it. Right now. Despite you being in a weakened state."

The boy merely arched his back and spread his asscheeks for the insertion of Meissner's hardening cock. The Nazi continued to rub soap and hot water over the boy's trim body, all the while maneuvering his cock further and further in the boy's hole.

Compared to the session he had just had with Roebling, this session was akin to lovemaking. The hot water fucked the two gently with its' invigorating spray. Meissner's cock slid in and out easily, with the added soap and water. Meissner, sensing climax, began a more vigorous pumping and rammed his cock hard into the boy's hole. The boy winced, but a smile was seen on his face. He flexed the muscles in his ass until the man's cockhead was caught inside. Bringing pressure on the shaft only accelerated the climax. The man spread his legs and with one final exertion, shot a load up the boy's ass. The hot jism, like the hot shower of water, renewed the boy. He was desperate to please his Master and would do anything needed to please him.

CHAPTER ELEVEN

Confession

The next three days were days of defeat for the Nazi Regime. A number of direct hits on munition factories. Fighting men killed on the battlefronts. Nazi planes lost. The mood in the compound was grim. Meissner increasingly sat in his office, ordering the evacuation of prisoners and trainloads of innocent victims to be executed at one of the camps.

A list of desirable men to be captured and interrogated had circulated among the Allied Forces and both Roebling and Meissner were listed for having committed human atrocities.

Meissner's only solace was to return home – if he was able to return home at all each night – and ram his cock down his American slave's throat or up his ass. It was rare that he was able to be serviced by his handsome Aryan youth at the office, with constant communiqués flooding in from all over the wounded Regime. Papers to sign. Decisions to make.

Between the two boys, however, Meissner's Leather boots were kept spitshined. He was always impeccably dressed in full Leather uniform. "Damn the Americans! We will defeat them yet... and turn them all into Nazi slaves," he thought. Deep down, he knew it would never happen. Roebling was right. He turned von Wiedering's proposal over and over in his mind. He enjoyed the power he felt as a Nazi. The fear he saw in the faces of the prisoners, the occasional cockiness of an enemy soldier. Much like Franz had been when first encountered. He admired their spirit but he mused, "It must be suppressed and squashed like a bug under my black Leather boots. Flicked off the wall like a fly with my riding crop." His cock rose at the thought of his boot firmly planted on the genitals of a captive soldier. Heaving, squeezing his eyes shut to alleviate the pain, an attempt at macho bravado by screaming, "Fuck You!" Still, the appeal of relocating to a plantation in South America, where he could pleasure himself with young, handsome men. Naked, under his control. Looking at him with respect... and lust. The American had told Meissner that he loved him. "Love?" Meissner smiled his sadistic smile, as he spit a bit of cigar leaf from his half-smoked cigar, "Fuck love."

A knock on the door and Roebling entered.

He sat in front of the desk and propped his booted feet on the desk.

Meissner offered him a cigar which he quickly accepted.

"Your boy Hans is disappointed in you, Meissner. He said you seem terribly distracted."

"Too much fucking paperwork to process." Meissner complained.

"I took him into the storeroom and fucked him... so that he would not be forgotten."

"Fuck you, Roebling. He is my aide. He should only be taking cock from his Commandant."

"He said he hasn't had your cock up his ass in at least four days. Hasn't even sucked your cock once."

"Damnit, Roebling. We are in crisis. I have more important things to think about than fucking a boy."

Roebling merely clucked his tongue as he shook his head. He drew several strong puffs on his cigar.

He lowered his voice to a whisper, "I've decided to take the offer of our friend. We leave in five days. I have my equipment, and drew out money from the bank accounts I have here. You must come with us, Meissner. Think of the pleasures that would await us. A fuckboy every day of the week. Punishing naughty boys – surely you like that idea."

Meissner was sweating – he knew that he had to confess to his old friend Roebling.

"Let's discuss it tonight at my apartment. Come about 2100 hours if you can."

"Jawohl, Meissner."

Meissner stewed about his impending confession all afternoon. He was short-tempered with every aide that entered his office to deliver more communiqués, more paperwork, more directives. His mind continued to turn over the offer of von Wiedering. If Der Fuehrer was victorious, he would be one of the upper echelon – far-surpassing the role his Father had played in the SS. He would be respected and feared throughout the Aryan nation and the world, for that matter. What if Roebling was right? Roebling was his mentor, having helped him rise quickly through the ranks. Roebling had never steered him wrong during his early days in the SS.

A knock sounded on the door. It was Johann, one of the aides.

"Mein Commandant, we have an unruly prisoner. Herr Bilinkoff thought you might be the best officer to take care of him."

"Bring the scum in, boy."

The prisoner was escorted in by two guards. One of the guards held him in a choke-hold around his neck.

He was a large man. It was obvious he had held a position of authority-his clothes were expensive. He glared at Meissner. He spat at Meissner, but it fell short of its goal.

"What's you name, prisoner?" At first, the prisoner remained silent.

The guard tightened his choke-hold on the prisoner's neck. "Answer the Commandant, you swine," the guard insisted. The other guard kneed him in the groin. The man flinched in pain.

"Wilhelm Metzger," he finally replied.

"And what crime has he been imprisoned for?"

The guard replied, "For making derogatory statements against Der Fuehrer and for other officers of the SS."

"What have you been saying, Metzger?"

"That you're a bunch of faggots. Der Fuehrer being the biggest one. Fuck any male ass you can find."

"I assure you, Metzger, there's at least one that we have no desire of doing that to." Meissner laughed at his own sadistic joke.

He opened his desk drawer and pulled out his revolver.

"Turn the prisoner around." The guards maneuvered Metzger around with some struggling involved.

"Lower his pants." Metzger was struggling but he was no match for the beefy guards. His fat ass was soon revealed.

"Looks like you have eaten well, Herr Metzger."

"I'm a successful businessman, you fucking pervert. I know the right people. I socialize with the elite of society. I don't bugger males. My friend Heinrich Himmler is sseeking out perverts like you and you will be eliminated. You're just a worthless ffaggot," Metzger said, as he began to stutter

"I've been called worse by lesser shitheads than you, Metzger."

He held the revolver in the asscrack of Metzger's amble ass.

"You ever had a man's cock up your ass, Metzger."

"I have not, I'm normal. Not like you, you are an abomination. We know your practices – you brand a desirable young man with a pink triangle and then you have his way with them. Sticking your member up their ass. You'll roast in hell for your wicked ways. Sssomeday you'll pay for your sssins."

Metzger stuttered even more as beads of sweat appeared on his forehead.

"Looks like we are not the only ones with imperfections, you fat ass."

"You let me out of here, I have mmmoney. I know im – im – important pppeople," the prisoner continued.

Meissner pressed the revolver further into the ample asshole.

The cold metal of the revolver must have chilled the prisoner as it inched up the hate-filled man's asshole.

Meissner ordered the guards to strip the fat swine. He had several packets of money taped to his body. Although the guards laid the packets of money on Meissner's desk, he indicated to them that they should divide it in half.

"Now, Metzger, you have no money." He ordered the guards to turn the prisoner around.

He was disgusting. Rolls of fat tumbled down his belly, hiding his shriveled-up cock.

"Doesn't look like you would make a very good SS officer, Metzger, you have no cock," the Nazi taunted.

The guards laughed, slapping the fat ass a couple of times with their gloved hands.

"Devil's spawn. Ffucking f-ffaggots," Metzger continued to yell, as sweat rolled down his forehead "You're not a man. I'm a m-mman. I started a business. I mmmade a great success of it. Then, you and your pack of perverts took over the country. This great country was f-ffounded on the principles of decent, honest, respectful mmen like my my my ssself..." The prisoner ranted on for some time.

"Shut the fuck up!" Meissner yelled as he savagely slapped the human turd across the face. He spit in his face. Meissner motioned with his revolver to have the guards rotate the prisoner once again, turning the prisoner's face away from Meissner.

"Metzger, for crimes against Der Fuehrer and for my fellow officers who you have slandered, I am sending you to a place where you no longer have to witness the supposed atrocities we are committing against handsome young Aryan men with their tight asses and hardened cocks, their muscular pecs and their delicious tongues which enjoy sucking the cocks of powerful SS officers." With that, Meissner placed the cold steel against the stuttering man's head and pulled the trigger.

"Get this garbage out of my office." Meissner ordered the guards as he rubbed the crotch of his breeches. He returned to his desk chair and lighted a cigar.

He yelled for his young Aryan. The session had made him desirous of the male sex that the disgusting Metzger had outlined. "Been accused of it, so I may as well follow through..." Meissner thought.

Buchner appeared and he motioned for the boy to stand against the wall. He pulled down the boy's trousers and without ceremony, shoved his cock, which had swollen to a respectful size, into the boy's willing hole.

He reached around and unbuttoned the boy's shirt. He began squeezing the boy's nipples with intensity. The boy moaned as his LeatherMaster pinched each of his boytits. The pain felt delicious.

"Thank you, Master. I was beginning to think I was in your disfavor."

As he thrust his cock in further, he replied, "This is your just punishment for telling Roebling of our lack of activity... you are my aide, no one's other. Your ass must pay the price."

He thrust with a ferocity as the boy flattened his body against the wall.

"You are never to tell another officer of our activities, boy. Am I understood?"

"Yes, Sir, Mein Commandant. My apologies. I deserve this, Sir."

"Damned right, you do, boy."

He continued to fuck the boy's ass until his cock was fully swollen inside the boy's Aryan ass. He ground it in further and released a load of jism from an over-excited cock. He withdrew his dripping cock and pulled the boy down to his knees. The boy was ordered to suck the man's cock clean.

Hours later, Meissner departed the office and returned to his apartment. The naked boyslave was kneeling in the dark.

"We have a guest coming. I must prepare you for him." Meissner retrieved a Leather hood from his closet and placed it tightly over the boy's head. "This will lessen the surprise for Roebling."

He laid out several wine glasses and retrieved two Cubans.

Roebling arrived promptly at 2100 hours.

The boy, for the moment, was secreted in the bedroom.

Meissner offered his guest a glass of wine and the men settled on the sofa with their freshly-lighted cigars.

"Roebling," Meissner began, "you know I have always admired you for your strength. You have served as my mentor and I will always be grateful for that. I...have to confess something to you."

"What?" blurted out Roebling.

"I have been keeping a boyslave here." Meissner got up and retrieved the hooded boy from the bedroom. The boy knelt before Roebling with his arms behind his back.

"Ah, the supposed nephew of an old friend, no doubt?" Roebling eye's twinkled.

"Nein, Roebling."

Meissner took several long gulps of his wine, pouring another glass for himself and refilling Roebling's glass.

"Who, then?"

Meissner took a deep breath and mumbled, "The American."

"What the fuck? The one Der Fuerher ordered you to execute?"

"The very one."

"Meissner, are you insane? That is treason."

"What can I say, Roebling. He was a good fuck. I've enjoyed fucking him every day since I captured him for my own use."

"Mein Gott, Meissner, if anyone ever finds out, you will be hung. Let's dispose of him before that happens. I'll help you."

"Nein, there is something different about him. I admired his spirit, his unwillingness to submit. I've been thinking about von Wiedering's proposal. The three of us...," began Meissner.

He was pre-empted by Roebling. "Fucking him is one thing, Meissner, secreting him out of the country without Der Fuehrer finding out is quite another matter..."

"von Wiedering would help us."

"I'm not sure I want any part of this. Granted, he was a good fuck."

The boy had maneuvered on the floor so that he was on all fours. His ass was presented to Roebling.

Despite his protest, Roebling cock had made an appearance in his Leather breeches. "I guess it wouldn't hurt to try out the boy once again."

Roebling unbuttoned his breeches and leaned over the boy. His cock was drawn to the boy's hole. He spread the boy's asscheeks with his gloved hands and soon was pumping his cock in and out of the proffered hole.

Meissner sat on the edge of a chair and unbuttoned his Leather breeches. His cock was inserted in the boy's open and willing mouth.

A frenzied mansex session was soon in progress. The boy's willing holes took both cocks. His ass expanded and contracted to take Roebling's full cock while his mouth swallowed the whole shaft of Meissner's cock. The men's riding crops were alternately slapping the boy's back.

The Leathered men were pumping, in and out, in and out. Meissner held the boy's jaw firmly in place, while Roebling was slapping the boy's asscheeks with his gloved hands.

Roebling's Leathered thighs were squeezing the boy's asscheeks as he pumped more furiously. Meissner's head was arched backward as the cock disappeared into the boy's mouth. Riding crops slapped the naked flesh of the boy's back. The boy's ass arched upward as Roebling's cock thrust in and out, in and out.

The boy's mouth sucked hard on Meissner's cock. He vacuumed it as his ass clamped shut on Roebling's cock.

Roebling shot first, followed very closely by Meissner.

Jism poured out of the boy's mouth and ass. He tongued the jism off his Master's cock. His ass continued to expand and contract holding Roebling's cock captive until the final drops of jism were greasing his rectum.

Finally, both Leathermen pulled out. Meissner collapsed against the back of the chair. Roebling flopped onto the sofa.

"All right, Meissner, we will take the boy with us."

CHAPTER TWELVE

Flight

The next morning, Meissner reported to his office at the scheduled time. The usual pile of papers was on his desk for action to be taken.

He had only been working for twenty minutes or so when Roebling rushed into his office, unannounced.

"Well, Roebling, what brings you here so early? Good mansex must mean you slept well..."

"This is no time for levity, Meissner. I have just received word that Heinrich Himmler is on a rampage. He has announced a cleansing of high-ranking officials who are suspected of homosexual activities. He is personally confronting them, allowing them to confess, and then, executing them on the spot. We need to get the hell out of here as fast as possible. It is my understanding that he is approximately 170 kilometers from here. He plans to do a sweep of this area by early this afternoon. We only have several hours to evacuate."

"Surely, he wouldn't include us, Roebling, we have been loyal to Der Fuehrer."

"I heard that he publicly stated that Der Fuehrer is no longer capable of making decisions and that he will make the decisions for the Reich."

"Shit!" Meissner replied.

"I have faked orders stating that we are headed to Bergen-Belsen at Himmler's request to interrogate suspected SS officers. We must leave now. We will pick up your boy and your belongings and head to von Weidering's.

"Fuck, Roebling, if we get caught, we will be executed."

Roebling only nodded in agreement as Meissner retrieved a box of Cubans and they headed for Roebling's sedan which was parked out in front of the compound.

They both nodded to the guards who were unaware of their diverted mission or else they would have been restrained by the same guard who had reported on Meissner's indiscretion.

As they headed to the highway, Roebling filled Meissner in on the latest communiqué from von Wiedering which indicated a willingness to take the American boy to South America. By the time they arrived, he would have necessary fake identification papers for him to travel with the Nazi officers. Just the trip to von Wiedering's was dangerous – there were a number of roadblocks. The men would have to sound convincing in their lies if they were to successfully reach von Wiedering's.

The drive to the apartment seemed excruciatingly long, but finally they arrived.

Meissner hurried into the apartment only to find the boy confused at his appearance so early after his departure. "We must leave now," Meissner stated, "I will explain later. Get into the Nazi uniform you wore when you first arrived here."

Meissner hastily packed some of his most precious Leathers, including his items of pleasure-torture and as many pairs of his boots as he could stuff in a substantial duffle bag. He had the presence of mind to obtain a large amount of cash prior to the morning in question. He reached into the secret bureau compartment and retrieved two more boxes of Cubans.

The boy hastily dressed, but was having difficulty getting his feet in the boots. "Put them on in the sedan. Hurry."

He rushed out onto the street, making sure that no one was loitering nearby and rushed the barefoot boy into the waiting vehicle.

The three sped off, situating the American in the back. Meissner was seated with him. Their gear was discreetly placed in the boot of the car.

They passed a number of military vehicles, headed the other way. Several were sedans with the Nazi swastika emblazoned on the doors. They avoided the gaze of the drivers and the occupants of the vehicles as they sped further and further away from the compound.

They had driven approximately thirty kilometers when they encountered the first blockade of the road.

A soldier held up his hand for them to stop. Roebling wound down his window.

"Sieg Heil, Mein Commandants," the guard saluted.

"Sieg Heil," they all three said in strident voices.

"What takes you away from the compound?"

"Direct orders from Himmler," Roebling replied.

"Do you have the papers, Mein Commandant?"

Anticipating the request, Roebling clutched the forged papers in his gloved hand.

The guard examined them for several minutes, looked into the emotionless eyes of Roebling, and waved them through.

They breathed a collective sigh of relief.

The second blockade, approximately twenty kilometers beyond the last, was more of a test.

The guard examined the papers much more carefully, examining the faces of the three Nazi soldiers.

Roebling and Meissner remained calm, but a bead of sweat appeared on Franz's forehead.

"The soldier – why is he accompanying you?" the guard inquired.

"We needed an aide to process some of the paperwork. Franz is accomplished at many tasks that will aid us greatly in the expedition of the same," Meissner hastily explained.

"All right, pass through, Mein Commandants. Sieg Heil," the guard saluted.

"Sieg Heil." Yet one more stumbling block had been successfully hurdled.

Roebling continued the journey, passing into the remote villages of northern Germany. The going was slower – the roads were dirt, pockmarked with potholes.

To calm their nerves, Meissner pulled out his cigar case and extracted three cigars. He handed his clip to the boy who clipped one for each of the officers and finally one for himself.

The sedan was soon filled the aromatic smell of the Cuban cigars. Meissner began rubbing his crotch. The smell of cigar smoke served as an aphrodisiac for him. He rubbed the American crotch.

Roebling, catching the action out of the rearview mirror, upbraided him, "Not now, Meissner, plenty of time for that later... at least, we hope."

The sedan drove through more villages. The villagers paid little attention to the sedan. They had seen more than their share of Nazis in the past several years. In fact, they gave the vehicle a wide berth. The villagers hid their secrets in barn lofts, basements, behind false walls. An underground had developed for the safety of each village. Brother pitted against brother. There was little, if any, trust among neighbors. Your neighbor might be the next informant.

The sedan headed into even more remote areas, where houses were nestled into the hillocks of Germany.

The vehicle often had to slow as farmers herded their cows to an adjoining field, blocking the road.

Approximately seven hours later, the three Nazis pulled into the courtyard of von Wiedering's home in Neumunster.

Within several minutes of their arrival, von Wiedering hurried out the front door. Like his Nazi counterparts, he was dressed in full Leather. His hands were encased in tight black Leather gloves. He wore spitshined, knee high boots.

He embraced the two men and shook hands with the American.

"There is no time to lose. I am packed. I have already shipped a number of my art objects and torture devices to Copenhagen at an exorbitant price. But I have received word that it has been shipped aboard a safe ship which the Allies will not bomb. It will take several months for it to make its way to South America. Hopefully, we will be happily situated there before it arrives."

"And what of your boys?" Roebling inquired.

"I have placed all but one. He has expressed a desire to be my boyslave in South America. I will be taking him along."

"Now, let's get your vehicle unloaded and then we must destroy it, giving your former Nazi brothers one less clue as to where you are."

The gear was unloaded and the men re-entered the vehicle. They followed von Wiedering in his Duesenberg to a remote location of the property, within a grove of trees. von Wiedering had prepared for the occasion. He lit a fuse from a great distance. The men raced to his car and retreated as quickly as possible.

Before they reached his home, a load explosion and a great ball of fire lighted the afternoon sky.

The men retreated to the compound. It looked oddly forlorn without the many artworks on display. Most of the furniture remained in place, however.

They sat at the dining room table. The boyslave Tomas, the one who had chosen to remain behind, brought them a plate of cold lamb, vegetables and a half loaf of bread. A bottle of wine and glasses were already on the table.

von Wiedering had a packet of information for each of them. The packets contained their false identification papers.

The false identification papers announced that they were Danish doctors, returning from a medical conference which focused on genetic engineering. One of Der Fuehrer's favored topics for creating the Aryan race. They were headed to their base of operation in Copenhagen and then immediately leaving for another medical conference in India. Hopefully, it would fool any curious guards. von Wiedering reviewed their false identities. After reviewing the papers and wolfing down the meal, von Wiedering explained, "You will have to pack your Leathers carefully away. You can no longer appear as officers of the SS until you are once again in safety – South America."

Reluctantly, the men stripped off their comfortable Leathers, uniforms they had worn so proudly for the past several years. Both men felt oddly naked without the comfortable Leather breeches caressing their thighs and their Leather shirts and jackets rubbing against their easily-aroused nipples.

von Wiedering stripped too. Tomas presented the men with outfits more suitable to men of the aristocracy – well-tailored suits, fedoras, silk hosiery, and wing-tipped shoes.

"Well, Meissner, you clean up well," Roebling taunted.

"Shut the fuck up!" Meissner retorted as he slipped his riding crop inside his suit jacket.

"We will leave in one hour, heading for Copenhagen. We then head to an extended flight until we finally reach Bombay, India. I know this seems odd, but we must avoid any flight zones patrolled by the Allied Forces. I have secured the services of an excellent pilot and co-pilot. They have been paid more than a king's ransom to fly us to safety. From India, we sail to Australia. From Australia, we travel due east for an excruciatingly long journey aboard ship until we finally arrive in Argentina. All told, we will not see my new home for another two months. If we get there at all." Up until this time, von Wiedering's voice exuded confidence. The confidence lagged as his voice trailed off during the last two sentences.

A nervous tension was now in the air. The men sat in stony silence as the minutes went by agonizingly slow.

"Sir," Tomas re-entered the room, interrupting the silence, "the hour of departure is at hand."

The four men were escorted to the Duesenberg. Tomas was dressed in livery appropriate to a chauffeur. The men's gear was stowed discreetly throughout the luxury car. von Wiedering stood for a long moment looking back at his compound. It would be the last time he viewed it. His mind flashed back to the many pleasant, and wickedly painful, sessions that had taken place in the dungeon, in the bedroom, in the secret chambers. With a wistful sigh, he climbed into the back of the Duesenberg and Tomas shut the passenger door.

They headed off into the gathering darkness.

CHAPTER THIRTEEN

Execution

As the Leather Nazis were speeding toward von Wiedering's compound, Himmler was checking off men who were confronted, made to confess, and executed. His check list was marked with blood-red "Xs' as he confronted a number of SS officers suspected of engaging in homosexual activities. As he headed toward the compound commanded by Meissner, he was particularly interested in Meissner's confession. Word had reached him that Meissner had shot an old friend of his, Wilhelm Metzger. Revenge was in order. Metzger had contributed a large amount of money for the good of the cause. Himmler had given a good share to the Reich's coffers, but had pocketed an equal amount. He had also heard that Meissner had a strong interest in young Aryans. And not for their military prowess, but prowess at being fucked.

It was several hours before they reached the compound.

Himmler's driver opened the sedan for Himmler and he climbed out.

The guards snapped to attention and shouted, "Sieg Heil!" He returned the salute as he marched into the office.

He found Meissner's office empty.

"Find Meissner," he barked to the aide who appeared at Meissner's door.

"Sir, he left several hours ago with Commandant Roebling."

"Oh?"

"Jawohl, Mein Commandant."

"Where did he go?" demanded Himmler.

"I do not know, Sir."

"Well, find out, asshole."

Himmler sat at Meissner's desk, leafing through the papers left on Meissner's desk. All seemed in order as he then rifled through Meissner's desk.

The aide escorted Hans, Meissner's aide, into the office and closed the door behind him as he left.

"What's your name, boy?"

"Hans Buchner, Sir."

"Buchner, where is Commandant Meissner."

"I do not know, Sir. He left this morning with Commandant Roebling."

"I already know that, asshole."

Himmler got up from the desk and walked around it to confront Buchner.

"Tell me all you know, boy."

"I have told you, Sir, Commandant Meissner came in at the usual time this morning. Commandant Roebling entered the Commandant's office and they left shortly after. They departed in Roebling's sedan."

"What time did they leave, boy?"

"It was approximately 0900 hours, Sir."

Softening his approach, Himmler questioned, "Buchner, was the Commandant good to you?"

"Oh, yes, Sir, very good, Sir."

"Did you ever do favors for him, Buchner?"

"I did whatever he told me to do, Sir."

"Did you ever do sexual favors for him, Buchner?"

"What do you mean, Sir?"

"Did you ever suck his cock, boy? I speak perfect German, and you know damned well what I mean by sexual favors." Himmler was becoming impatient with the boy.

"Ur...," the boy stuttered.

Himmler slapped him across the face.

"Yes," the boy blurted out.

"What else did you do for him?"

"I... allowed him to fuck my ass and mouth with his cock, Sir."

"Do you know, boy, that that is against the rules of conduct, boy?"

"Yes, I suppose it was, Sir," the boy stated. He began trembling and tears rolled down his cheeks.

"This amounts to a confession, boy."

"I was doing as ordered, Sir."

"Did you protest when he was fucking you?"

"No...Sir."

"Did you enjoy it, boy?"

"Not at first, Sir. But I came... to anticipate it as part... of my duties." The boy was heaving as he spoke.

Himmler sat at the desk, found a blank piece of paper, scribbled several lines on it, and scratched a line with the boy's name printed beneath it.

"Sign this, boy." He thrust the pen into the boy's trembling hand.

"I was...only... doing as the Commandant commanded, Sir."

"We do not tolerate sex between men in the Reich, boy."

The boy scribbled his name. More tears were rolling down his cheeks.

"Stand against the wall, boy."

The boy was trembling as he walked with leaden feet to the wall.

Himmler unbuttoned his holster's flap, drew his revolver, and stood squarely behind the boy.

"You are a stain on the SS and must be eliminated." With that, he shot the boy once in the head and the boy's body slumped to the floor.

Himmler kicked the boy's body. He removed the swastikas from the boy's lapels.

"Human garbage" was Himmler's final remark as he exited the office.

He marched outside to the sentries.

"Were either of you here when Commandants Meissner and Roebling departed?"

"Jawohl, Mein Commandant, we were both here."

"Which way did they head?"

"East, Sir."

"What did they have with them?"

The Commandant was carrying a box of cigars, Sir."

"What was their conversation as they departed?"

"They did not speak, Sir."

"Were they acting in an unusual manner?"

"Not particularly, Sir."

"In the last several weeks have you noticed any unusual behaviour?"

The guard was only too glad to tell about the 'nephew' that had escorted Meissner late one night.

"Where were they headed?"

"Well, it was 0200 hours, Sir. I can only assume they were headed to Meissner's apartment."

"Write down his address."

The guard had to check records inside but soon returned with the address.

"Dank," said Himmler as he saluted the guards.

Himmler motioned for his driver to open the passenger door. Himmler climbed inside and ordered the driver to head east.

He fumed. That bastard Meissner always seemed one step ahead. And now Roebling, a well-respected officer in the SS, was implicated with Meissner.

"Two for the price of one when I catch up to them. I want to execute them personally," he thought as the sedan headed east.

As he fumed, he urged the driver to drive faster. "If we don't get there soon, your ass will be the next transported to Dachau. Now, get me there SOON!" Himmler became angrier as the minutes ticked by.

Despite the increase in speed, it still took them thirty-five minutes to reach Meissner's apartment.

Himmler banged on the door and not receiving an answer, shouldered the door and prepared to force the lock. Instead, he found the door open. He and the driver, both armed with revolvers, quickly searched the apartment for Meissner. Everything was in order – there were rinsed breakfast dishes on the sink, the bed was made, bath towels neatly folded on the shower door. Himmler stalked angrily back into the living room. A closed desk was in the corner of the living room. He jimmied it open with the knife on his belt. Recent bank withdrawals. A forgotten snapshot, showing Meissner and Roebling in full uniform. They were standing with a distinguished looking man wearing expensive Leather clothing. Behind them six young men, all of whom appeared to be naked. On the back a penciled inscription was written. It read, "Too bad you couldn't spend a whole week. J. von W." A trash can was nearby with several ripped up pieces of stationery. Himmler did not take time to piece them together, but pocketed the financial documents, the photograph, and the discarded writings. After sweeping through the apartment one more time, he angrily left the apartment.

He ordered his driver to convey him to Berlin, where Der Fuehrer might provide him with some clues to the whereabouts of Meissner and his accomplice Roebling.

CHAPTER FOURTEEN

The Leather Masked 'Ball'

Tomas drove most of the night. Fortunately, the men did not encounter any blockades until they reached the Danish border. It was heavily armed with German soldiers, who were on high alert. As the Duesenberg approached the guards, von Wiedering exited the vehicle and approached.

"Good Evening..." he began.

"State your business," the guard retorted, cutting off any attempt at civility.

"We are doctors returning from a medical conference at the request of Der Fuehrer. We are returning to Copenhagen."

"Papers."

"Certainly," von Wiedering responded, approaching Tomas' rolled-down window and accepting the sheaf of faked identification papers.

The guard glanced at the papers and returned them to von Wiedering. "You will have to wait until 0800 hours tomorrow morning. We are instructed to let no one through. Executive orders from Heinrich Himmler. At that time, he will issue a listing of any clearances for vehicles crossing the border."

"But surely, we can pass... Der Fuehrer himself commended us for our work on genetic engineering. As soon as we return to Copenhagen, we must prepare for a similar conference in Bom... er, another medical conference."

He realized that he should not share any details with the guards that he might later regret.

"Nein. I suggest you return to your vehicle and wait until 0800 hours. No exceptions."

Despite the fact that he wanted to spit in the guard's face, he thanked him and returned to the Duesenberg.

"Shit," he muttered as he closed the door of the vehicle. He explained the situation to the passengers.

"What if Himmler catches up to us?" Meissner questioned.

"How would he know where we were headed. He has surely searched your apartment by now. Can you think of anything you left behind that would provide a clue?" Roebling queried.

"Nein, I have been careful not to mention our visit to von Wiedering's estate."

Franz was increasingly nervous as he thought about the letters he had drafted and then ripped up. They expressed his love for Meissner and thanked him for saving him from execution. Did he mention their future plans? "No," he thought silently to himself, I was just beginning to write that when Commandant came home unexpectedly. I ripped up the letters at the point. But why didn't I take the letters with me?"

"Well, we might as well retreat and find someplace to stay for the night. Get a good meal," Roebling suggested,

"Ask the guard."

von Wiedering once again got out of the Duesenberg and ambled over to the guard, "I know you are not a travel bureau, but is there a place to eat and to stay the night?"

Pointing in the direction opposite from which they came, "Ten kilometers."

von Wiedering thanked him and returned to the vehicle. Tomas drove slowly away.

They reached a respectable-looking eatery. The staff looked dismally at them as they entered. Not another soul was in the eatery. They sat at a table, pointing Tomas, the chauffeur, toward the kitchen. Someone finally came over and presented them with menus, although many of the selections were crossed out, with "Not available" written across it.

The three men were accustomed to living well, but had to settle for soup and roasted potatoes. The eatery did have a selection of wines and so, two bottles were ordered.

They ate silently as it seemed the whole staff was watching them.

The meal ended quickly and they then asked if there were rooms available nearby.

The waiter replied, "Fifteen kilometers to the only place in the area that has not been closed down by wartime. Most places have been commandeered by the German soldiers. I cannot guarantee that it has not been closed down as well"

Red flags went off in the heads of the men and they mutually decided that they would spend the night in the car. Pulling off the main road.

They had a fitful night. "Mansex would be good," Meissner thought briefly, but even he was not interested.

The sun rose over the horizon and the men headed back to the border blockade.

The guard approached the vehicle. "We have received a listing of authorized vehicles and yours' is not among them."

"Surely, it must have been overlooked. Would you please look again?" von Wiedering politely requested. All three of the men were ready to jump out and overpower him.

The guard scanned the list, rechecking the vehicle's registration. "Nein, nothing."

"Sir," von Wiedering countered, "would it be possible for you to telephone our hospital in Copenhagen and confirm that we need to return?"

"We have no telephone lines here."

"What about a telegram?"

"The nearest telegram office is forty kilometers away and we cannot leave our post."

"What if we went to the telegram office and had it forwarded to you. Would that suffice?"

"Nein, orders from Herr Himmler only." The guard walked back to the sentry post and watched them carefully.

The men conferred. Meissner said, "I'd like to take my boots out, put them on, and ram them up his arrogant ass."

Roebling concurred, "I'd hold him while you did it."

von Wiedering was thoughtful, "Tomas, drive away, drive in the direction we came."

After several minutes, von Wiedering exclaimed, "DAMN! Why didn't I think of this sooner? We have wasted so much precious time with that fucking fool."

"Tomas, we need to proceed to Maasbuell. It is perhaps five or ten kilometers east of Flensburg. We're going to pay a visit to Herr Johan Eckener."

"Who the hell is he?" questioned Roebling.

"Surely, Roebling, you have heard of the Eckener family? Hugo Eckener – pioneered German zeppelin aviation? Johan is his cousin. A very rich man. And... the Master of one of my boys. Shit, why didn't I remember sooner? I sold him... wait, what was the boy's name?... he was my Tuesday boy two or two and a half years ago. He lives only ten kilometers or so from the Danish border. He can get us across without any guards bothering us. We have wasted so much time!"

With that, the men's spirits rose. Little did they know that Himmler had conferred with Der Fuehrer and now knew the identity of J. von W., a wealthy man who was now seriously in trouble with the likes of Henrich Himmler, the true Commandant of the Third Reich.

As Himmler exited Der Fuehrer's headquarters, he thought "I will now execute all three. Cut off their genitals and send them to the Der Fucking Fuehrer, the ignorant asshole."

He entered his transport vehicle and ordered his driver to drive non-stop to the estate of Johan von Wiedering in Neumunster.

Tomas had followed von Wiedering's directions carefully and they were now headed to the outskirts of Flensburg. The men were in much higher spirits.

Meissner reached over and cuffed Franz on the head.

"You have said very little during this trip, Franz." Franz looked miserable.

"Oh, Master, I have done something for which I am so sorry."

Meissner who had been on the brink of a smile, returned to his normal, sour expression. "What? Tell me immediately before I throw you out of this sedan."

Franz told him about the discarded letters.

"You asshole, I ought to turn you over and fuck your ass right now."

Roebling interceded, "Hold on, Meissner, all Himmler would have to do is to speak to Der Fuehrer. Der Fuehrer would quickly tell him about our interrogation of Franz and where it was held. Himmler undoubtedly knows. By tomorrow morning, the guards will be on the lookout for four men traveling to a border. We just hope that Herr Eckener can secrete us across the border without border patrols breathing down our necks."

Franz felt somewhat better with Roebling's conversation, but looked at his LeatherMaster with tears in his eyes.

"I'm sorry, Mein Commandant, I have let you down. If you want to throw me out, I will not resist."

"Oh... fuck it," Meissner finally said, "but you will receive severe punishment for it."

"Thank you, Master."

The journey continued but they were soon in the small town of Maasbuell. von Wiedering was unsure of the exact location of Herr Eckener's estate – he had only been there once. His instincts, which were usually correct, eventually guided them to the Eckener compound. Built in the 1740s, the house resembled a castle. They pulled into the courtyard and three large mastiffs came charging at them. Soon, a handsome man came out to the Dusenberg. He yelled 'Silence' to the mastiffs and they obeyed.

von Wiedering emerged from the car and raised his hand in greeting.

"Mein Gott, is that you, von Wiedering?" Eckener questioned. He, much like von Wiedering when the Nazi officers first met him, was dressed in full black Leather. Tight black gloves and knee-high boots complimented his Leather shirt and pants. His belt had two riding crops attached to it. He was younger than the Nazis anticipated. He was a man of only twenty-seven or so.

"It is indeed. How are you, Herr Eckener? Are you taking care of our boy?"

"I am fine and he is fine. But, what? Have you brought me a whole crop of men?"

Meissner explained the situation. Fortunately for them, Eckener was not of the Nazi party and was not sympathetic to it.

Eckener waved the men to come inside. They were grateful to do so. The house was immense with thirty-seven rooms, heavily laden with carved, gilded furniture and foreboding portraits of Eckener's ancestors.

Eckener rang the servant's bell. Soon the boyslave made his appearance. Much like von Wiedering's boyslaves, the boy was naked except for his wrist restraints.

"Master, how may...," the boy paused as his eyes recognized von Wiedering.

"Master?" he questioned.

"Yes, boy, it is your former Master. You are looking fit, boy. But your present Master called you."

"Yes, Sir, please forgive me, Sir," the boy said, as he lowered his head.

"That's all right, boy, I completely understand your surprise. I am surprised too. Bring several bottles of wine and some fresh fruit and cheeses. I'm sure the gentlemen are hungry."

"Herr Eckener, I must admit... I cannot think of your boyslave's name...," von Wiedering confessed.

"Manfred"

"Manfred, of course. I was thinking he served me on Tuesdays... Mondays, of course, how forgetful of me. But, where are my manners? We have intruded on your household and I have not even told you who these gentlemen are."

He felt that he could trust Eckener and so, he presented them with their true identities.

"Men, I 'm very glad to know you. I cannot say that I support what you stand for... or that is to say, what you stood for... but I am only too happy to help you."

Manfred reappeared with a silver tray fully laden with the requested food. The men were ravenous and devoured it like it was their last meal.

"I'm sure that you would like to relax, freshen up. I do have to tell you that I have a small party scheduled for tonight."

"Oh, Herr Eckener, I am so very sorry for us just barging in...," von Wiedering said.

"Not at all, not at all. In fact, I would like you to join us. I know you would fit right in, if you understand the unspoken, von Wiedering?"

"What? Is it related to our pleasures, Eckener?"

"Well, you can make up your mind, but the invitations said that it is a masked Leather 'ball'. And, von Wiedering, I don't dance." The men laughed easily for the first time in many days.

"But, Herr Eckener, the only clothing we have are these repulsive suits," Meissner complained, "and our SS uniforms."

"Hmmm," contemplated Eckener, "I think I can outfit you. I even have some masks. That way, you won't know who you are fucking."

"Damn," Roebling said, "I like your idea of a party."

Several hours later, the Duesenberg had been hidden away where no one could find it. Eckener had led the way to his Leather closet. Row upon row of pants, shirts, jackets, breeches, and boots.

Meissner and Roebling quickly selected their outfits from a selection with military bearing. Tomas and Franz wisely chose leiderhosen, however, these were outfitted with the buttoned cod in the rear. Both slaves knew what their roles would be that evening and might as well be prepared for it!

The guests began arriving shortly thereafter. Handsome man after handsome man. The Masters appeared in full Leather, the slaves in minimal Leather. When all the scheduled guests had arrived, Herr Eckener announced that he was hosting several unexpected guests and that they should be made to feel welcome. And they were. Groped. Caressed. Squeezed. Rubbed.

Roebling, Meissner and von Wiedering were not shy. Each targeted several young slaves, swiftly escorting them into a darkened corner for some long-overdue exploration of a young Aryan body. Tits were pulled. Asses were squeezed. Cocks were rubbed. Assholes were pried open. Bodies collided. Black Leather against male flesh. Nazi officers, once again encased in Leather, were worshipped by Aryan boys. The Masters were not shy about seeking out the newcomers. Power struggles ensued until a cock was pulled out and it was shoved down a willing throat or up an accepting ass.

At 0100 hours, Eckener clanged a large dinner gong. The newly-arrived Leathermen were mystified as to what it meant, but the invited guests were not. The boys lined up against the wall of the hallway. Their asses were exposed as the boys arched their asses upward and presented them for 'inspection'.

Tomas and Franz joined the line-up. At the same time, the Masters, including Roebling, Meissner and von Wiedering, lined up against the opposite wall, with their cocks hanging out of their pants. At the sound of the next gong, the Master at the head of the line led the way to the opposite end of the boys. He inserted his cock in the asshole of the boyslave. A ten minute interval ensued and then the Masters moved up the line. All wore masks in order that a Master did not favor his own slave, although Eckener acknowledged that a majority of the Masters would recognize their own slaves by their naked asses or another desirable attribute. It just added to the festivities of the evening. If a Master so desired, he could paddle or flog a boy to arouse himself into climax.

The Master to cum the most times (Eckener was the judge) was declared the 'Ball' Master for the evening. It was simple in its set of rules but gratifying for most of the participants. Meissner, Roebling, and von Wiedering took every advantage to stick their cocks up a willing boy's hole. This celebration was like a dream come true. As was the usual case, Eckener himself was participating and he lost track of who came when. And so, as usual at Eckener's parties, every Master was declared the 'Ball' Master and every boy was declared the town whore. Masks were discarded as each Master and slave retreated to a bedroom, the fucking continued well into the next day.

CHAPTER 15

In Hot Pursuit

While the Nazi officers slept well into the day, Himmler's entourage had driven through the night. He had arrived at von Wiedering's estate by mid-morning. There was obviously a lot more to sift through for possible clues, but it was obvious that there were no humans in residence. Remains of a meal were evident in the dining room. The shadows of framed items appeared on the walls throughout the house. The basement was strangely empty, but it was evident that substantial wooden devices had been removed. Himmler went on a rampage, ripping open drawers, scattering superfluous material to the left, to the right, over his shoulder.

"Damnit," he exclaimed, "I want those bastards and I want them now."

Thinking that von Wiedering might return, Himmler ordered that the estate be burned. Gasoline was found in the motor shed. The guards spread it liberally over the carpeting, soaking the drapes and bed clothing throughout the house. One of the guards fashioned a fuse out of a rope also found in the motor shed. One end was placed in the gasoline can and the other extended out through the front door.

Himmler himself lit the match. They watched the 'fuse' burn for as long as they dared and then scrambled to the safety of the entrance gate.

"Fuck you, von Wiedering and your traitor bastard friends. When I catch up with you, you will wish you had expired in this fire."

Himmler ordered his entourage to head to the Danish border. It seemed a logical place for anyone trying to escape the country.

The two Nazis had slept peacefully after a delicious night of mansex. Fucking boys restored their energy and their hope that they would soon be on their way to Argentina.

They dressed in the loaned Leathers and headed downstairs. Men and boys were slowly making their way into the dining room. The masks were off. Masters were still in full Leather, their boys who stood submissively behind their Master's chairs were appropriately naked. Franz, who had slept in Meissner's bedroom, stood between Roebling's chair and Meissner's chair. von Wiedering's Tomas stood behind him. Eckener sat at the head of the table, Manfred knelt behind his Master's chair.

"I trust, men, that you had a memorable night..." began Eckener.

Masters' heads nodded, paying tributes to their host for such an enjoyable party.

A toast was proposed.

Eckener continued, "We need your help. The gentlemen that you met last night are in great need of getting across the border without... supervision of the border sentries... even though they were members of the Nazi party, they are part of our 'brotherhood' and must be helped. Talk among yourselves. Enjoy the meal. I will reinstitute this conversation at the end of the meal."

The men were literate, professional men with many diverse interests – although they uniformly enjoyed the pleasures of the previous night. Some were German, some were Danish. Although the conversation covered many topics, the men agreed that they had a solution for the problem presented by the host.

Roebling and von Wiedering resembled two of the Danish men in the group, Meissner, Tomas and Franz more closely resembled three of the boyslaves in the group.

Meissner balked at the idea of looking like one of the boyslaves.

"You want to live, don't you?" von Wiedering questioned.

The men at the party would simply trade identities with the Nazis and their boys. After they were safely across the border, their identity papers would be brought back by a mutual friend.

"Solved. Thank you, men," Eckener said, "And now we really should send our friends off to their appointment in Copenhagen."

The five reluctantly went back upstairs to redress in the suits.

The Dane who was lending his identity to Roebling also offered the use of his sedan. It could be returned once they were safely in Denmark. Eckener assured von Wiedering that his Duesenberg could be stored at his place until such time he could retrieve it.

The men's personal items were stored in the Dane's car. The men said their goodbyes, expressing their gratitude to Eckener and they were on their way.

Arriving at the border one hour later, they breezed through without a hitch. A spark of recognition lighted the guard's eyes, mistaking Roebling for the Dane who had graciously lent his identity and his car.

Once in Denmark, the men breathed a slight sigh of relief, but, of course, Denmark was under Nazi occupation and there were still dangers. They had to arrive safely in Copenhagen.

Himmler glanced back from the safety of his sedan. Flames were leaping from the first floor to the second floor. A heavy cloud of black smoke rose toward the sky. He smiled a sadistic smile and chuckled to himself.

The journey took longer than anticipated because the road system was unimproved – dirt roads with deep ruts. Farmers herding their cattle or sheep across the road. Himmler was more impatient each time a slow-down occurred. Rolling down his window, he cursed at the farmers. They virtually ignored his tirades, although one farmer came rushing at them with his raised sickle. Himmler pulled out his revolver and shot at the farmer, but missed.

The caravan continued heading north.

Finally, Himmler reached the Danish border. He questioned every guard at length.

"Nein, no one like that has attempted to cross the border while I was on duty," the guard replied. The other guards concurred. "However, Herr Himmler, you may wish to interrogate the guards who are here in the late evening-early morning hours. They will be here in about two hours."

Himmler waited. The guards arrived at the sentry post and were told that Himmler himself was waiting for them. They made their way quickly to his sedan.

They were asked the same questions as the other guards.

"Well, yes," the guard replied, "there was a Duesenberg..."

"That's it! What did the occupants look like? Did they give you any information that might be useful? Did you let them through?"

The guard described the chauffeur and the older man. "The older man was very affable," Mueller stated. He became less affable when Mueller, the guard, would not cooperate. He didn't really get a very good look at the three men in the back seat. "No, to answer your question," Mueller said, "I did not let them through. They came back and tried to go through again. Saying they were medical doctors heading to Copenhagen."

"Three men in the back seat? Chauffeur? Who the fuck are they?" Himmler screamed. "Wait, think," he thought to himself, "Roebling, von Wiedering, Meissner. von Wiedering was rich – he probably did have a chauffeur. But who the hell was the fifth man?"

"Copenhagen, huh?" Himmler replied.

"That's what they said, but when they finally left, they headed west. Copenhagen is due northeast of here. My guess is that they headed to Flensburg. They will try to weasel themselves across the border at the sentry post there. The sentry has already been warned. Not everyone drives a Duesenberg."

Eckener was only too glad to have some guests stay longer than anticipated. It meant that there were several cute boyslaves and handsome Masters to play with. Manfred was a very attentive boyslave, but Eckener liked variety once in a while. After all, each boyslave had talents unique unto himself and as a good host, Eckener rationalized that he should know those 'talents'.

It was a beautiful day and Eckener had invited the remaining guests to sun by his swimming pool. He had only recently had it installed and was anxious to see nearly-naked men lounging around it. In the buff, Manfred took drinks for orders. As the men were sunning in the lounge chairs, Manfred handed out the drinks. His substantial dick hung alluringly over each man's mouth and hands. Several couldn't resist pulling on it.

"Manfred, I need to talk to you," said Eckener.

"Yes, Master?"

"Can you take the car, run into town, and get something to feed our guests for this evening's meal?"

"Well, Sir, there is a problem. Your vehicle has two flat tires. I have tried to patch each tire with scraps of rubber, but the scraps just are not big enough." Wartime shortages were evident even among the wealthy. The items were simply not to be had.

"Hmmm..." Eckener thought, "I don't know where we have any more rubber in order that we can patch the tires. Shit! ...Oh, but wait, I'm sure that Herr von Wiedering would not mind if we took his Duesie out for a little mission."

Manfred dutifully left. Most of the stores in town were devoid of any groceries, let alone a precious commodity like meat. Manfred remembered that there was a farmer who would sell Eckener freshly-killed chickens (for an exorbitant price). He lived southwest of Flensburg. It was a beautiful day and Manfred wanted to take advantage of it. Driving a Duesie. King of the Mountain.

Manfred drove to the farm. Parking the Duesenberg, he politely knocked on the door.

"Good afternoon, Herr Straub. I am inquiring as to whether you have any chickens that you would be willing to part with to make a tasty meal for some guests from Denmark."

"I do have three that I was saving for next Sunday. But if these are for Herr Eckener, I guess I will part with them. They will be succulent. The feathers are a thing of beauty, with a sheen of golden highlights on each feather. Ah," he sighed, "it's a pity that you can't eat the feathers too."

"How much, Herr Straub?"

"Oh, for my good friend Johan Eckener, twenty Reichsmarks... each."

"What? You could buy half a house for that!" Manfred exclaimed. Of course, he was exaggerating. But the price given for the three chickens was also an exaggeration.

They dickered. Finally, they reached an agreeable price. Herr Straub slaughtered the chickens and even plucked them before handing them to Manfred.

As Manfred headed back to Maasbuell, he noted that a caravan of cars was swiftly approaching him from the rear.

He speeded up. The caravan kept pace, edging closer and closer to him. He noted that the sedans were proudly displaying the Nazi flags, but he didn't panic. They were probably traveling to Flensburg.

Himmler was impatient to reach Flensburg when the driver alerted him to the fact that there was a vehicle in front of them.

"Sir, it looks like a Duesenberg."

"Get closer. Don't loose him."

As they pulled up behind the vehicle, it was indeed a Duesenberg.

"How many fucking Duesenbergs can there be? It's an American swine vehicle. Manufactured by an ex-patriot of the German state," Himmler thought to himself.

Manfred continued to travel to his Master's compound. As he took the road which led to his Master's estate, the Nazi vehicles followed. He didn't know what else to do. He led them straight to their intended target.

He pulled into the yard. The Nazis jumped out and surrounded him. His hands were tightly pulled behind his back.

Himmler got right up in his face and demanded, "Who lives here?"

"My Mas... uh, Johan Eckener."

"Who else is here?"

"Some Danish friends are visiting."

"Who are they?" Himmler demanded.

"I'm... not sure of their names."

"Lead us to them."

Manfred struggled but was no match for Himmler's aides.

Manfred led them to poolside where the naked men were engaged in poolside fucking.

Himmler yelled, "You are all under arrest for committing acts against the rules of the Third Reich!"

The men scrambled to stand up. Eckener was among them.

He strode over to Himmler, "What's the meaning of this? You are on my private property."

"And you, Herr Eckener, are a criminal for harboring Nazi traitors."

Guards, having emerged from the other Nazi sedans, surrounded each man.

"Well, well, well," Himmler crowed, "we've caught all of you... Meissner, Roebling, von Wiedering... aren't you a sight for sore eyes. Caught in the act of fornicating."

The men protested. Unfortunately, their similarity in features to the men who had escaped across the Danish border was their downfall.

"We are Danish citizens. We are not who you think we are."

"Prove it, liar."

The men looked at each other. They had sent their identification papers with the Nazis and von Wiedering.

Eckener tried to reason with Himmler, but Himmler was on a witch hunt and was satisfied that he had finally captured his intended prey.

"Tie them up!" Himmler ordered.

One of the guards retrieved rope from the boot of one of the vehicles. In quick order, the men were lashed together.

They were led into Eckener's home.

Himmler withdrew execution papers from his jacket and began filling them out. Johan Eckener. Karl Roebling. Johan von Wiedering. Gunther Meissner. He filled out the last order with great satisfaction.

He began questioning the remaining three, including Manfred.

While he was questioning the three remaining, the guards searched the house. There were no other people in the house.

Himmler unsnapped his holster, drawing out his revolver.

"For crimes against the Third Reich, you are hereby eliminated from the Reich as a stain to humanity." Himmler declared. One shot to each of the four men's heads as they slumped to the floor.

He ordered the guards to round up the three remaining men and lined them up against a wall.

Looking at his guards, he ordered them to take aim. All three men were shot and fell to the floor.

"I want the Duesenberg brought into the house. Accomplish the same thing you did at that traitor von Wiedering's house. I will be outside."

He marched out and the guards carried out his orders swiftly. Eckener's house was in flames when the caravan of Nazi vehicles left the estate.

CHAPTER SIXTEEN

At Sea

"This fucking trip is taking forever," Meissner complained.

They had been at sea for three weeks, with nothing but endless water in every direction.

"Herr Meissner," von Wiedering said soothingly, "soon, we will be enjoying the bounty of nature in our new compound. A bevy of young men to meet your every need. Every sexual need and every sadistic fantasy."

Meissner's cock rose in his pants as he thought of the adventures ahead. "Have we really gotten away with it?" he thought.

He went to his cabin where his American whoreboy was lying on the bed. When the door closed, Franz slipped to the floor and bowed his head.

"Master, I am here to serve you."

Meissner cuffed his head but he felt powerless without his Leather uniform. He pulled out his Leather breeches, boots and Muir cap. He felt restored with them on. He picked out his riding crop and began lightly flogging the boy. His steel blue eyes sparkled as a sadistic smile appeared on his face.

He began lashing the boy more vigorously. It felt so good to once again reassert himself as a powerful Master.

The boy's back was soon covered in lash marks.

The boy responded, "Sir, thank you, Sir."

"Take my cock in your mouth, boy."

The boy obliged. It had been a long time since he had a vacuuming from his American boy. The former Nazis had attempted to blend in to the rest of the passenger list, just in case there were Nazi informants. To the passengers on board, they were Danish physicians traveling to Argentina for research purposes. They had been very careful not to reveal their sadistic desires to anyone, yet.

He shoved his cock in and out of the willing boy's mouth. The boy stroked the shaft of his Master's cock with his tongue. Meissner came very quickly.

He was letting the boy lick his cum off his dick when a knock came on the door.

He placed his cock back in his breeches only to find Roebling wishing to enter.

"Ah hah, I had a feeling that your cock would stir soon. Don't deny it, Herr Meissner, the evidence is on your boy's lips. I was hoping to have a similar massage from your boy"

"Be my guest, Roebling." Meissner indicated as he pulled his own recovering cock from his breeches.

Roebling did not have to receive a second invitation. His cock was already rising in his expensive suit.

His cock throbbed as he pulled it out of the zippered fly.

The boy began a careful and slow sucking of the man's cock. Roebling pulled the boy's head closer and closer until the whole shaft was in the boy's mouth. The boy tongued the shaft and the head of Roebling's swollen member. Roebling, too, came very quickly.

The boy was licking Roebling's cum-soaked shaft when a knock was once again heard on the door.

It was von Wiedering.

He closed the door and announced, "Hitler is dead. He committed suicide. Admiral Karl Doenitz has been named President of Germany. Flensburg has been named the seat of the Reich government."

The look of surprise on the men's faces quickly gave way to looks of concern, and relief, and uncertainty.

von Wiedering continued, "It looks likely that the Reich will disintegrate."

Fortunately, for the men, everyone on Board was relieved that the War might soon be over. There was cautious celebration. The men and their boys joined the other celebrants on the deck. In honor of the news, the Captain had prepared a special feast for the weary travelers.

The men had only viewed one other ship on the journey and it must have had a fresh stock of fruit and vegetables. It had hovered near the men's ship and a supply boat was seen traveling between the two. It seemed all the travelers aboard had wearied of the food that was kept in the ship's larders. This was a welcome change.

Each passenger was given a small glass for a toast of champagne.

One young man caught the eye of von Wiedering. He was slender with a boyish build. His white pants revealed a muscular cock hanging down his leg. His torso was nicely defined and the striped polo shirt hugged his muscled chest.

"Umm, handsome," von Wiedering muttered to the other men.

"Umm, I quite agree," Roebling said.

"Like to see what's inside those pants."

"I'd like to see what's on the other side," said Meissner, willing the boy to turn around to reveal his ass.

The young man apparently sensed the men looking at him and strolled toward them.

"Good afternoon," he said.

"Good afternoon, young man," von Wiedering replied.

"Are you enjoying the celebration?" the boy innocently asked.

"Enjoying the view...," Roebling stated, his eyes undressing the boy.

"Would you care to join us?" Meissner asked, pulling out the chair next to him.

"Yes, gladly," the boy replied, "I don't really know anyone on board."

"Oh, well, let me introduce you to our table," von Wiedering quickly replied and proceeded to make introductions under their assumed names, of course.

"I'm Aaron" the boy said, "I'm Australian."

"What brings you on board for this long journey to South America?" Roebling asked.

"A new life."

"Oh? You weren't satisfied with the old life?" von Wiedering probed.

"Well," the boy seemed reluctant to continue.

"Come now, young man, you're among friends," von Wiedering said in a soothing, fatherly tone.

"I was in a bit of trouble in Australia and felt it in my best interests to leave."

"Oh, we like bad boys. Don't we fellows?" von Wiedering replied.

The men nodded in agreement.

Not wishing to continue, the boy looked toward the sea.

"We are headed for Argentina. I have a compound there. You'd be most welcome to join us until you discover what you want to do with your life," von Wiedering offered.

The boy smiled a shy smile, replying "That's very kind, but... well, I don't know."

He made motions to leave, but von Wiedering in his wisdom knew that the trap had been baited and the mouse would not be able to resist the cheese.

The boy thanked them for the offer and left the table.

The men continued to watch him as he circled the deck several times, staring off into the sea. Glancing back, looking at the men.

"Give him time, he'll be back," von Wiedering declared, "I just know it."

They continued to converse. The day was waning, but the late afternoon sky was flawless. The sun was beginning to sink below the horizon.

The crowd had thinned, people were retreating to their cabins. The men pulled out their cigar cases and handed their selected cigars to Tomas and Franz, who had remained silent for much of the time. The boys clipped the men's cigars and lighted them for the men.

"Damn, Meissner. I'm glad you had the presence of mind to retrieve your Cubans."

For the moment, the boy had disappeared from view, but he re-emerged on the deck some time later.

He glanced over several times. The men were watching him out of the corners of their collective eyes.

The men made idle conversation. The boy was glancing more frequently in their direction.

"I'd like to plow his ass," Roebling said.

von Wiedering replied, "I saw him first."

"You greedy bastard – you already have a boy to service you. And Meissner, you do too. Here I am, all alone and boyless."

The men chuckled at the attempted pathetic look on Roebling's face.

"Fuck you, Roebling, you just had your knob sucked by my boy," Meissner teasingly said.

"All right, all right. Roebling, you get first crack at the boy's ass," conceded von Wiedering, "And here is your chance. He's coming over."

The boy said, "May I join you?"

"Certainly, dear boy. Would you like a cigar?" von Wiedering asked.

"No, no thank you. I'd like to know more about your proposal."

"Well, this gentleman," von Wiedering started, pointing to Roebling, "can fill you in. We were about to take a stroll around the deck and enjoy the salt air."

The four excused themselves, leaving Roebling and the boy to converse.

They stood for a long time, viewing the gathering darkness. von Wiedering glanced over several times only to witness the two deep in conversation.

"Do you think he will succeed?" Meissner asked.

"You know him better than I do — has he ever failed in a conquest?"

"No," Meissner replied, with a sadistic grin on his face.

They continued to look out to sea, wistfully wishing that they would spot land. And that they were the one seducing the desirable young man.

von Wiedering nudged Meissner and stated, "His charms must be working, they have just disappeared downstairs."

Roebling led the boy to his cabin. He offered the boy a drink, which he gladly accepted.

The cabin was stuffy and Roebling took off his suit coat, untied his tie, and unbuttoned his shirt.

The boy watched him very closely.

A slight smile appeared on Roebling's face. "It is warm in here, isn't it?"

"Yes, yes it is," the boy replied. He downed the drink and Roebling quickly poured him another.

"Oh, no, no thank you. One was enough. That's potent stuff."

"This?" Roebling said, as he held up the bottle, "it's innocent."

"Oh, well. Maybe it's just me."

"Why don't you relax on the bed?"

"Oh, I really should be going."

The Nazi in Roebling made its appearance. "No, you are not going anywhere."

He stood over the boy and began massaging his rising cock in his pants.

"No, really, I should be going."

"You'll go when I say you go, boy."

"What? Listen, I..."

"Shut the fuck up, boy. I take what I want. And I want to see what you've got in your pants."

The boy protested as Roebling pulled the boy by the waistband of his pants. He threw the boy on the bed, holding his arms down.

The boy struggled. He was strong and Roebling had a difficult time holding him down.

He planted his mouth squarely on the boy's mouth. Despite his protests, the boy began moaning. His tongue responded to Roebling's exploration with his tongue. The boy could feel the hardening bone in Roebling's pants.

"Sir, really..." the boy struggled once again, gasping for air as Roebling's tongue thrust into his mouth.

"I want to fuck you, boy, and you will be my willing partner in that endeavor."

The boy continued to protest, but Roebling was a man who normally got what he wanted. He had not had good male sex in some time.

He reached down and pulled the boy's pants down around his knees.

The boy's cock was swollen, throbbing against Roebling's own rod.

"You must enjoy a big man on top of you, boy, or else your cock is lying to you."

"It's just that...," the boy started, "I'm a virgin."

"Even better, boy, because I intend to take your ass willingly or unwillingly."

"No!" the boy shouted.

Roebling slapped the boy roughly against the cheek.

"You will obey me, boy."

Roebling's cock was straining against the fabric of his trousers. With one hand, he quickly unzipped them and pulled out his engorged penis.

"Willingly or unwillingly, boy?"

"No, really..." the boy protested.

"Unwillingly, then." Roebling proceeded to slap the boy hard against the face. The boy's eyes welled up with tears.

The boy began to cry, heaving, trying to catch his breath.

"Calm down at once," Roebling ordered.

The boy got himself under control. Leaving the boy momentarily, Roebling retrieved two straps of Leather and tied the boy's wrists to the bedposts.

The boy watched, too frightened to react.

Roebling removed the boy's shoes and pants. He raised the boy's ass off the bed and positioned the boy's legs over his muscular shoulders. He rubbed his cock. It was now fully extended. Roebling inserted one of the boy's socks in the boy's mouth.

"This will hurt. But only momentarily. You will relax and take my cock up your ass. You will enjoy it."

The boy nodded, fear in his eyes.

Roebling rubbed the spit from his own mouth and jammed his cock up the boy's virgin ass.

The boy screamed into the sock.

Roebling pumped his cock hard into the boy's virgin territory.

Gliding in and out, in and out, pumping it in slowly, releasing it. Each time he thrust it in, his cock inched in a little further.

The boy continued to scream, but Roebling talked to him in a low voice. Reassuring him that he was doing well.

In and out, in and out. Further and further up the hole.

The man was clenching the boy's asscheeks, guiding his cock into the boy's fuckhole. The boy began moving his ass with the rhythm of his fuckdaddy. The cock was easing in and out, with a harder thrust each time it went in. Finally, Roebling's cock was fully inserted in the boy's hole. The Leatherman's balls slapped against the boy's asscheeks.

Roebling's head reared back as he slammed his ramrod into the boy's hole. Harder and harder. Both were sweating from the exertion. The Nazi continued to encourage the boy with his low, masculine voice. The boy was responding to the new experience. He was enjoying it – a slow smile spread on his face.

The Nazi could no longer control his cock. He rammed it in one final time and shot a load of jism.

The boy let out a gasp as Roebling's head flew backward, "FUCCCKKK!" he yelled.

They both were frozen in position for some time, Roebling heaving from the exertion. The boy relishing every minute that the man's cock remained in his fuckhole.

After some time, Roebling withdrew his cock. Approaching the boy, he ordered the boy to lick his cock clean. The boy tongued it with great eagerness.

"Thank you, Sir," the boy said between swipes of the tongue, "Thank you, Sir."

"You're welcome, boy."

And so the days passed on the high seas. Each man had a boy to fuck. Aaron indicated a willingness to become Roebling's boyslave, following the men to the compound in Argentina. There was free interchange of boys among the three men. Three weeks passed, finally reaching the coast of South America. von Wiedering had arranged for transportation. It looked as if freedom was close at hand.

CHAPTER SEVENTEEN

A New Home for Leathermen

One year had passed since the Nazis fled Germany. Their new home was an estate in Argentina. The home had the benefits of being extremely private and remote, but with access to many amenities. While at home, the former Nazis enjoyed all the pleasures of their former lives. von Wiedering continued as he always had. He had a network of connections throughout the world, which forwarded to him beautiful boys for enslavement. Training, discipline, sadistic pleasure, fucking handsome, naked boys.

Word had reached them that Himmler had claimed victory in their capture and execution. For all intense purposes, they were dead to the world. They liked it that way – they could continue doing what they always had done. And poor Himmler, "Fuck the bastard, he got what he deserved," mused Meissner, with a sadistic grin on his face. "It's a pity I couldn't have been there with my riding crop. I would have beat his ass raw. Even after he had committed suicide."

The views were spectacular. The three men always enjoyed breakfast on the new home's east terrace.

Their three naked boys – Tomas, Franz, and Aaron, all with Leather wrist restraints, served them their breakfast and knelt before them to shine their knee high boots. The Nazis always wore their Leather uniforms to breakfast. von Wiedering was always clad in full Leather as well.

The boys worshipped their handsome Leathermen. They were very proud of them.

"Good Morning, Herr Wiedering, and how is the Lord of the Realm this morning?" questioned Meissner.

"Good Morning, Gentlemen. We have a full day of activity scheduled. We are to receive six boys some time today and you will want to introduce them to our regime of discipline, I assume?" von Wiedering replied.

"I wouldn't miss it," Meissner stated, with an evil twinkle in his steel blue eyes.

Roebling concurred. He swatted his boy Aaron for missing a spot on his boots.

They finished their leisurely breakfast and re-entered the house. Herr von Wiedering's extensive art collection had arrived safely and now lined the halls and rooms of the estate. His favorite, *The Flogging of St. Paul,* appeared in the front hallway. The torture devices had arrived much later than the artwork but were now fully operational in the dungeon of the house. The men had tested many of the devices on their willing boys. Mitchell Franz was quite familiar with several of them, having been subjected to them when he was their American Prisoner of War.

The former Nazis went to their bedrooms and each checked his uniform in the full-length mirror. Muir cap pulled low over their intimidating faces. Leather jackets, shirts and neatly-tied tie, breeches, and of course, their spit-shined boots. Tight black Leather gloves stretched over their hands. Each had his own favorite riding crop tucked into the belt.

They were ready for action as they trooped back downstairs.

They did not have long to wait as two caravans pulled into the courtyard.

The drivers escorted the initiates out of the back. They were paid liberally and sent on their way.

The boys were all uniformly handsome. They were hooded and blindfolded, wrist restraints holding their wrists together behind their backs and ankle restraints around their ankles.

"Too many clothes on them – let's see what we have acquired," von Wiedering announced. He himself was wearing a red Leather uniform with black epaulets, pocket flaps and a stripe down each leg.

The three boys undressed the new recruits.

They ripped the shirts off, the boys wouldn't need those anymore. Their pants were also removed.

Six naked, handsome young men.

They were lined up against a wall. The wall had rings attached to it. The wrist and ankle restraints were quickly padlocked to the rings and then, finally the blindfolds and hoods were removed.

The boys blinked as the sunlight hit their eyes.

"Good Morning, boys. I am Commandant Meissner. I will be your instructor, along with Commandant Roebling who stands to my left. Herr von Wiedering, who stands to my right, will be your supervisor. You have been sent to us for training and discipline. You have been sent here to fulfill the dreams of many men throughout the world who wish to have a subservient boyslave."

The boys remained silent as they listened carefully to the Commandant's rules and regulations. Fear could be seen in their eyes.

The Commandants and von Wiedering approved.

Commandant Meissner then began interrogating each boy in turn.

"Name, boy," he asked each one. He then questioned them on their dick size when it was fully aroused. "Have you ever taken a cock up your ass? Have you ever taken a cock in your mouth?"

Most of the boys were very inexperienced. Only one appeared cocky and self-confident. He was led away to the dungeon where Meissner would work him over.

As he was manacled to the wall in the dungeon, Meissner hooded the boy once again.

His handsome muscular back and ass flexed as he attempted to wrest himself from the manacles.

"There is no escape, boy. You will submit to our sadistic pleasures."

The boy remained silent.

Meissner began an intense flogging with the riding crop. The boy flinched, but did not cry out.

Meissner realized that this boy was exceptional, able to take a great deal of pain. He silently counted out one hundred heavy flogs to the boy's reddening back and one hundred heavy flogs to the boy's ass.

The boy stood silently.

Meissner inserted two fingers and then three fingers up the boy's hole.

The boy's asshole expanded to receive the intrusion and soon, Meissner's fist was up the hole.

"Good boy," Meissner declared, as he rotated his fist within the boy's hole.

He withdrew the fist, withdrew his hardened cock from his breeches and slid his rod up the boy's hole.

The boy's hole easily accommodated all of Meissner's cock – head and shaft, right down to the loose balls.

The boy's fingers flexed, otherwise he remained motionless. His ass flexed and expanded as Meissner worked his cock in and out of the fuckshaft.

Meissner was becoming impatient, he liked it when a boy groaned, or arched his back, or otherwise indicated that the cockfucking hurt.

He pounded harder and harder into the fuckhole. The boy simply remained silent and almost motionless.

Despite the fact that he wanted to prolong this initiation, Meissner shot a load of cum. It was then that the boy rolled his head back, moaned, and slammed his own naked body against the wall. The boy's cock was fully aroused and a geyser of jism shot upward against the wall.

"That's better, boy." Meissner arched his right arm around the boy's neck, pulled the boy's head backward and said, "See that you react like that every time I fuck you."

"Yes, Sir," the boy replied.

"What is your name, boy?"

"Heinrich, Sir."

"Heinrich what, son?"

"Heinrich Himmler, Jr."

And so, the intense training of boyslaves began for this new crop of boys. The Leather Nazis flogged them, fucked them, and introduced the boys to the sadomasochistic pleasures that real men enjoyed.

ABOUT THE AUTHOR

G.W. Leatherman Parks

G.W. Leatherman Parks has been a Leatherman for over thirty years. He is a proud member of the Leather Archives and Museum in Chicago and writes frequently for FLAGSHIP, the newsletter of Fits Like a Glove. He has also been published in *Drummer and Cuir: For LeatherMen by LeatherMen.* He is a collector of vintage Leather, Leather artwork and photography.

This is G.W. Leatherman Parks' second book. His first book *Leatherdaddy* is available from Amazon.com, TheNazcaPlainsCorp.com or your local bookstore.

LEATHERDADDY

Erotic Literature by the Black Leather Gloved Hands of

G.W. LEATHERMAN PARKS

PARKS

LEATHERDADDY

A
BONER
BOOK

www.ingramcontent.com/pod-product-compliance
Lightning Source LLC
Chambersburg PA
CBHW051145260626
47170CB00005B/1966